Egg Heaven

Praise for *Egg Heaven*

Home to drifters, loners, and those people with the third eye who seek out and embrace the sorrows of others.

—Kathleen Alcalá, author of *Spirits of the Ordinary*

In Robin Parks's characters, in these finely wrought stories, we find a simple and decided and unflinching dignity and courage.

—Thomas E. Kennedy, author of *The Copenhagen Quartet*

These stories of loss, longing, sudden departures, and necessary reconciliation break the heart. But Parks's compassion for her characters bleeds through the wreckage of their lives; we are presented, ultimately, with a picture of healing and hope.

—Gina Ochsner, Flannery O'Connor Award winner, author of
The Necessary Grace to Fall and
The Russian Dreambook of Color and Flight

Rarely does a collection achieve what we find here: art that truthfully captures both the fragility and strength of human relationships. *Egg Heaven* is astonishingly satisfying.

—Maureen O'Brien, author of *B-Mother* and *The Other Cradling*

Parks has captured the dilemmas of folks perched on the continent's western edge and treading the brink, always en route in an effort to sate the hungers they can name as well as those they cannot. These are stories of restlessness fed by emptiness, the kind that can starve a soul.

—Renée Ashley, author of
Because I Am the Shore I Want to Be the Sea

The hunger that runs through these vividly written, nuanced stories is beyond satisfaction by the food served in the diners and small eateries that serve as settings. It's the far deeper hunger of these characters for a home or a family or a connection with another that reveals their true cravings.

—Walter Cummins, co-publisher of Serving House Books,
editor emeritus of *The Literary Review*

Egg Heaven

Stories

Robin Parks

Shade Mountain Press
Albany, New York

Shade Mountain Press
P.O. Box 11393
Albany, NY 12211
www.shademountainpress.com

Parks, Robin
Egg heaven : stories / Robin Parks
ISBN 978-0-9913555-0-1 (pbk. : alk. paper)
California, Southern—Fiction.
Diners (Restaurants)—Fiction.
Waitresses—Fiction.
Working-class—Fiction.

Also available as an eBook
Printed in the United States of America by
    McNaughton & Gunn, Inc.

17 16 15 14   4 3 2 1

Stories in this collection have appeared in the following publications: "Home
On the Range" in *Prism International* (2000); "Las Golondrinas" in *Carve
Magazine* (2001), also *Best of Carve Magazine* (2002); "Egg Heaven" in
Connotation (2010); "La Playa" in *The Raven Chronicles* (2005); "Breakfast"
(titled "Restoration") in *Philadelphia Stories* (2006); "Delgado's Family
Mexican Restaurant" (titled "Bad Math") in *Perigee* (2008); "MarDel's Diner"
in *Paradigm* (2010); "Northwoods Tavern" (titled "Women, Bears and Other
Dangerous Things") in *Carve Magazine* (2001), also *Best of Carve Magazine*
(2002).

The author and publisher gratefully acknowledge these generous
donors for their major financial support of Shade Mountain
Press: Pedro Cabán, Heather Burns and Kathleen Maloy, Mary
Hood, Rubén and Moraima Morales, and Paul Navarro.

Shade Mountain Press is committed to publishing literature by
women.

In Memory of Sharon Sievers
1938–2010

Contents

Home On the Range

Penny placed her palm against the cool, dirty window of the bus, steadying herself as the Greyhound shuddered to a stop in front of Sherman's Feed and Seed. The driver pulled up the creaking parking brake.

"Twenty minutes, folks."

The door clattered open and fresh air swirled around Penny's face. When she drew her legs up to tie the frayed laces of her sneakers, her stomach gripped and heaved. She held still, waiting for the spasm to subside. She hadn't eaten since she boarded in Bakersfield, since Al had shoved that last rock-hard pumpernickel bagel at her with one hairy hand, the other shaking in her face as he nagged her not to talk to strangers on the bus.

Penny chewed her fingernails and held her stomach, which was whining like a sad dog. She would have to lift some food at this store. She gauged the distance between the bus and the wooden porch in long-legged footsteps, about six. She'd have to time it right, wait till just before the bus took off for the open road.

To kill time, Penny took out the map Al had given her and spread it across her blue-jeaned knees, trying to guess where she was. She'd lost track about twenty stops ago, maybe since crossing the California border.

Black bagel crumbs rested in a crease from the Pacific to Albuquerque. Al's fat pencil marked the rest of the route to New

York, ending in a curlicue and an arrow leading off the continent into the Atlantic, where Al had written "Eugenia" but had crossed it off and written "Ruth" and an address in Brooklyn. He couldn't remember his cousin's name, or which cousin he was actually remembering, but that didn't seem to dampen his belief that the cousin—Eugenia or Ruth—would take Penny in with open arms.

Penny licked her finger and blotted up the crumbs. She doubted she would make it all the way, but it didn't really matter. She didn't believe there were any cousins there anyway.

A telephone line sagged from the store like an empty clothesline waiting for someone to come home. Further away, a tiny flash of lightning against a low brown hill caught Penny's eye. Then a rumble of thunder. She knelt on her seat and pressed Al's Brownie camera against the window, waiting for the next streak. Above the hill now, a bright fracture in the sky, and Penny began to count, "One-chim-pan-zee-two-chim-pan-zees." Through the viewfinder was the southwest—maybe Texas, which was halfway to Kansas City, halfway again to New York, as Al had explained.

"Whatsa matter with you!" he had shouted over the high counter, waving his spatula, rocking back and forth on his feet, laughing. "Don't you know anything? Ha!"

They were having one of their endless trivia battles and Penny fumbled when Al asked where the Midwest began.

"Big deal," she said. "So I don't know where the goddamn-mid-fuckin-west is. *You* can't *spell* worth *shit*."

"Oh yeah? Shit? Ha! S-H-I-T!" he bellowed, flipping an egg right off the stove. It landed on the floor. No wonder customers never came back.

And it wasn't just the yelling and how the little diner—Home On the Range—was always out of things, like mustard for the pastrami and sugar for the cornflakes. It was the service, too. Somehow Penny and Al had gotten into the habit—during slow periods, which was just about always—of playing Scrabble and pretending not to notice when customers came in, sharing an unspoken hope that the customer would give up from lack of service and leave them to their game. Even after two years, Penny was still surprised when a customer just wouldn't give up but sat patiently, five, ten, even fifteen minutes until Penny couldn't stand it anymore and would call over her shoulder, "Coffee?," rising with exaggerated fatigue, as if her eighteen-year-old back had seen better days. She hated leaving Al alone with the Scrabble board. He cheated, looked at her letters, moved *s*'s around on the squares.

The biggest fight they had ever gotten into was over Scrabble. The Santa Ana winds had blown hard for three days straight and there was no one in the diner the whole time but Penny and Al. They were in the middle of their fifth straight game. Al had heaped a plate with french fries, garlicky dill pickles, and boiled eggs, balancing a monkey dish of Thousand Island on top. They sat at their little table halfway between the door and the kitchen, hands dipping into the food in turns like oil derricks, concentration high. Al hunched over the playing board. Penny could smell the Brylcreem he raked through his salt-and-pepper hair, faking a shower, his humped nose sweaty and sprouting wires. He breathed hard, snorting sometimes like a horse, rocking on his hips from too much energy, or coffee.

Penny had a word for the red triple score square and she was going to win again. She lit a cigarette to break his concentration as he rubbed his cheek—smoother than it ought to be for a man of sixty, Penny thought again. Must be all the booze. Works like a preservative.

Al covered his mouth with his thick fingers, black lowering brows shading his eyes as he studied the wooden tiles.

"Ah!" He nodded suddenly. "Aha!"

Al spread his arms out, then slapped his hands together, rubbing them fast. He coughed. He sucked his teeth.

"Come on, Al, just put the goddamn word down."

With his pinky finger extended as if he were picking up a teacup, Al delicately placed his tiles—M-I-T-Z-V-A-H—across the red square so that the *z* landed on a double letter score. "Ten! Twenty! Thirty! Plus—"

"It's a foreign word."

"What?"

"It's a foreign word! You can't use foreign words."

"What the hell are you talking about!" Al shouted, his mouth and eyes perfectly round. "Mitzvah! Mitzvah! Since when is mitzvah a foreign word?"

"It's not English! I don't know what it is, but it's not English. It's not even a word, far's I can tell!"

"Not a word? Not a word? Oy vay!" Al stood up, hands pressed against his temples. "That's it! I've had it!"

He flipped up the board. Beige tiles bounced off the table. A *v* disappeared into the pink dressing.

"Goddamn goy says mitzvah isn't a word!" He stomped away from the table. "Skinny little gentile waitress thinks she knows!"

Penny lit another cigarette, not noticing the one already burning in the ashtray.

Al threw a cup. It bounced twice, then shattered. He pulled at his hair as he strode up and down the diner, shouting at the ceiling. "Lousy bit of eighteen-year-old trash calls *me* a foreigner? Tells me *mitzvah* is not a word? Un-fuckin'-believable!"

"Would you quit yelling!" Penny followed him in circles. "I'm just telling you, it's not English!" She reached for the pitcher of ice water, but thought better of it. She sat back down at the table, trying to calm things down. She didn't want him to fire her again. It wasn't so bad when the weather was cool, sitting out on the porch, counting the wild desert lilies out by the road, waiting for Al to change his mind. But the winds outside were carrying debris from the road—scraps of paper, pebbles, dirt—in horizontal gusts past the screen door. While Al yelled that he knew what for, Penny imagined sitting by the side of the road, covering her eyes, the wind piling up sand along her body like a dune.

"It's just a game, Al," Penny said to Al's back as he went for the Smirnoff's in the refrigerator.

Al turned and planted both hands on the table, leaning over Penny. "Look it up." His nostrils flared out and in, his eyes were rimmed red.

"Fine." Penny went into the kitchen and pulled the enormous maroon dictionary from the lower shelf where the gray plastic bus trays sat empty. Al breathed hotly over her neck.

"Spell it again?" Penny said. Al's sweat smelled spicy, like cumin and fresh oregano. The smell floated over her cheek as she turned the thin pages.

"Ha! There! See? Right there!" Al's stiff, blunt finger pounded the page. Penny read aloud: "One, a commandment of the Jewish law. Two, a charitable act."

"Was I right? Was I right?"

"Yes, Al, you were right."

"Goddamn right I was right!" He snorted. "But you didn't think so, did you? You think I'm a stupid foreigner!"

"I didn't say—"

"Stupid, eh? Foreigner, eh? And after all I done for you?" Al started to make snuffing sounds and wiped his eyes. He reached into the refrigerator and took a long swallow from the bottle, then paced out of the kitchen. Penny followed.

"Don't take it so personal, Al."

"After all I done for you, taking you in, giving you this good job." Al went for the broom.

"Give it to me." Penny reached for the handle.

He pushed her away. "To hell with you." He bumped around the chairs chasing chips of white ceramic and blond tiles like mice. Penny followed.

"Show me the photos, Al," Penny said, prying the broom from his hands. "Go on, Al. Get the photos."

He looked wildly up to the ceiling, rocking back on his heels. "The photos?"

"I'll clean up."

"Yeah? Really?"

Penny swept while Al lurched up the stairs to his room above the diner. She heard each footfall, thick and hard, as he grabbed his photo album and another half-full bottle of Smirnoff's, this one warm.

When he came back down the stairs, Penny felt tired of being grateful. She needed to get the hell out. She had been there far too long. The night she'd arrived at Al's seemed like a century ago. She was sixteen then and had been hitching Highway 58 for days, trying to put distance between herself and the foster family who thought she was their state-appointed slave.

That night she'd kicked her way out of a yellow T-Bird and rolled beneath a juniper bush, shivering until dawn, until the blue neon of Home On the Range sprang to life and she smelled burnt toast. She crawled out from beneath the bush. The *n* in "Range" hummed dimly and steam rose from the roof as she approached the diner. She looked through the screen. A big gray-haired man in a sauce-stained shirt sat at a small table, looking up at her, a fork full of potatoes poised in midair.

"Whaddya want?" The food disappeared into his mouth, his dark eyes fixed on Penny while he chewed. Penny's stomach growled so loudly they both looked down.

"I'll clean up here if you give me something to eat." Penny picked scratchy leaves from her long hair while Al looked around the diner.

He pointed his fork at her. "You saying I'm dirty?"

Penny turned to go.

"No, no! Whatsa matter with you?" he said, rising, opening the screen door. "Cantcha take a joke? Eh? Here. My name's Al."

He took her hand in both of his, huge and warm and slightly slippery.

Penny swept the dining room. She dragged the garbage can out to the dumpster behind the diner. It was full of empty bottles and flies and reeked of dead animals. She washed all the dishes and pots and pans. When she mopped the bathroom floor, she tried not to notice the holes where the roaches fled.

By the time she finished, the sun was setting. Al put a plate of deep-fried chicken livers and a slice of plain rye bread in front of her. He brought her a glass of water. Penny ate slowly. Finally Al came out of the kitchen wiping his hands on the cotton towel that hung from his belt. Penny pulled her sweater around her and stood up to leave. Al said, "Thanks," and held the screen door open for her. As she walked out he turned the sign to CERRADO.

Penny walked out to the highway. It was almost dark and there were no cars in sight. She stood on the edge of the road with her arms crossed, kicking at rocks, a desert breeze lifting her hair. Later, when the moon rose, Penny sat down in the dirt and wrapped her arms around her knees.

An hour after dark, Al came out and got her. He led her up a staircase behind the restaurant, not the interior set of stairs she'd seen him use throughout the day. At the top he opened the door to a little room and snapped on the light. The room was empty except for a narrow cot covered with an army blanket. On the floor next to the cot was a jar of water with a lily in it. Al said he couldn't keep the diner clean himself, she was like a godsend, would she stay, rent free?

Sherman's Feed and Seed was one square building covered with laths the color of elephants. Penny watched a thin old man with a thick waist, white short sleeves and an ecru Stetson come out of the store into the now bright sun. He squinted and cupped his hands to light a pipe. After a few deep draws, he looked skyward. The nut-brown skin of his neck and bare arms hung loose with wrinkles. He kicked at a clod of dirt with the toe of his moccasin. The bus driver came around the side of the building, zipping up his fly.

Penny folded up Al's map and put it on the seat next to her. She sidled out of her seat and went to the back of the bus, into the lavatory cubicle. The heavy metal door slammed behind her and the stench of disinfectant and dirty diapers washed over her. Penny bent her head over the toilet, vomiting nothing. She wet the end of her shirttail in the sink and wiped the corners of her mouth and her forehead, then pulled her shirt out all the way, making sure it hung over the pockets of her jeans. She looked into the greasy mirror.

"I'm no thief," she had hissed that first week when Al had finally caught her stuffing saltines into her knapsack on her way out the door. "No one eats these old things anyway."

They struggled in a tug-of-war with the knapsack.

"Give it to me!" he yelled. "What else is in there, eh? Cash? The till?"

"No, nothing! Let me go!" Penny yanked on the bag and Al lost his balance, falling forward onto his knees. He was drunk again, his eyes wandering in different directions.

"Why do you steal from me, huh? Why? Why do you have no respect?"

"I told you, I'm hungry. Don't take it so personal."

Al groaned and lowered himself onto the cement floor. "Why do you have no respect for your elders, eh? What, you have no manners? How can you take things without asking?"

"You are not my elder, Al. You're my boss."

"Yeah, lucky me."

Penny turned to leave, the saltines falling to the floor.

"No. You cannot go yet. I want to show you something."

Penny sat down. She pulled the purple metal ashtray over and lit a cigarette while Al went upstairs. She heard his creaking footsteps above her head. He came back down the stairs with a bulky book tied with kitchen string under one arm, a pair of wire-framed bifocals dangling from one ear. He set the book down in front of Penny and patted it twice.

He went into the kitchen and reemerged with a plate of cold knishes in a puddle of congealed brown gravy, carrot sticks protruding from the sauce, and a cold bottle of Smirnoff's and a shot glass. He set the food down in front of Penny and sat down, pouring himself a shot. He adjusted the bifocals. Both lenses were scratched like a skating rink in winter.

Al made Penny look at every page in the photo album, which was filled with blurred and underexposed photos of women in babushkas holding babies, sets of children with Al's nose, young men with foot-long sideburns.

Every time Penny asked who someone was, Al got mad. "I told you. Family."

"But *what* family? I mean, who *are* these people?"

Al licked his fingers and gulped a shot of vodka before turning the page.

"Family. I told you." He burped.

"But where *are* they? Russia?"

"Russia, yes." Al peered through his glasses. "No. Not Russia. Ummm—" He licked his finger and turned a page. "Brooklyn. I dunno. Queens, maybe."

Penny had a vague suspicion that Al had found the album in a Goodwill store somewhere along the way, carting it with him from one failed enterprise to the next, East Coast to West. She was just about to ask when he turned from the photos and fixed his gaze on her.

"Quit staring," she said. "It's rude."

"Why are you so skinny, huh?"

"Leave me alone." Penny stood up.

"No, no. Sit down here like a civilized person. Now why don't you spend your tips on food, eh? Why don't you eat?"

"What tips, Al?" Penny shouted. "There aren't any goddamn tips because there aren't any goddamn customers! And why the hell would there be, huh? You tell me that!"

"Okay, okay! Don't get so mad!" Al waved his hands in front of her face. "I'm just saying, from now on all you gotta do is ask. Is that so hard, Penny? Quit acting like a crazy person, stealing and starving and wasting away. Now eat." Al shoved the plate of food toward her and resumed his careful turning of pages, sipping the clear liquid until the bottle was empty.

By the last page Al's eyelids drooped. Penny got up to leave, to go outside and around the diner to the back stairs. She stopped at the screen door and turned to watch Al begin to make his drunken way up the interior stairs to his room.

"You see, Penny?" Al stopped, shaking his head. "You don't steal from family." He disappeared up into the dark, one step at a time.

Well, Al, not to worry, Penny thought into the mirror. No family here.

She went back to her bus seat to check her knapsack for change. She thought maybe Al might have slipped in a few coins along with his camera. The olive-green canvas bag was empty of everything but two pencils and a used Kleenex. No money. Al couldn't afford more than her ticket, she knew that. They hadn't had a customer in weeks and most of the food turned to gray-green rocks in the walk-in.

"I've got to get out of here," Penny had told him over mashed potatoes and gravy so shiny with grease that rainbows swam around the plate. "I'm going crazy doing nothin' day after day. I've gotta work. I've gotta do something with my life, Al."

"Fine. Mop the floor."

"Al."

He looked up from his plate, chewing his meat slowly, his brown eyes moist like cow eyes.

"What?"

Penny tried to talk Al into selling Home On the Range and going back to New York. She told him there had to be opportunities there. For both of them.

"You go, Penny," Al had murmured. "You go find my cousins. They'll like you, though you're still too skinny."

In the end, Al said he'd buy himself a ticket south, try selling tacos from a little cart on the border. They closed the diner early and walked up the highway to the bus depot. Al argued with the ticket clerk about the weather in New York. On the way home, Al ducked into a little store and came out with a long whip of black licorice hanging from his mouth, a box of Milk Duds for Penny.

Six steps exactly, just as she thought. The darkness inside was cool. A tall skinny man loomed above the register, poking at the keys with one finger. Penny dusted her palms along huge burlap bags of seed and soil, and caught the clerk looking at her.

She turned down an aisle with shelves of Sen-Sen, pipe cleaners, and Zippo lighter fluid; toilet paper and gauze and Brylcreem lined the other side. Penny took a tube and twisted the cap open. She squeezed a little onto her finger, put it to her nose and closed her eyes for a moment. She put the tube back on the shelf and turned the corner, listening to the clerk talk with the bus driver.

"Not too bad here, no. But out there at the foot of the rise, that's where it'll getcha."

"Well, I welcome a break in these evil winds, that's for sure."

Penny turned down another aisle.

"Won't rain slow you down?"

"Yeah, but this is the milk run, you know? Folks on this bus are in no hurry, I can tell you that."

The aisle was filled with candy. Penny gently touched the wrappers of Abba Zabas and Mars. She thumbed through a deep stack of pink and black Good & Plenty and another of Red Hots. Her mouth watered as she plucked a miniature box of Milk Duds from the shelf. She glanced around. No one in her aisle. Quickly she palmed the small box and stuffed both fists into her pockets. She ducked around the back of the aisle and headed toward the light at the door. She almost made it.

"Miss!" the man behind the counter yelled. "Come on over here now."

Penny froze. "Damn," she whispered, facing the bright sunshine just a step or two away. Her fingers tightened around the Milk Duds. She turned to face the clerk.

"What?" She glared at him. He had faded blue eyes and stubble on his chin.

"Whatcha got in your pocket, huh?" He grinned menacingly. The bus driver snorted.

Just as Penny was going to tell them to go to hell and make a run for it, a voice from another aisle said, "She's with me, fellas." In a puff of pipe smoke, the old man in the Stetson stepped from one of the aisles and gave Penny a little shove toward the door. She ran out and climbed up into the bus, looking nervously back over her shoulder. No one followed.

Penny made her way through the bus. She dropped into her seat and watched the store from the window. Her heart pounded. The candy box poked her hip.

She pulled the Milk Duds from her pocket and tore open the pale yellow box, her mouth filling with saliva. She popped one into her mouth just as the old man came out of the store, cradling a brown paper bag like a football. The driver was right behind him. When Penny heard them board the bus she hunkered down into her seat. She held her breath as footsteps approached. The candy melted into a sweet river down her throat. Penny stretched her legs across both seats. She closed her eyes, pretending to sleep.

"Hey, Missy." She heard him just above her. She opened her eyes and saw him leaning over the back of the seat in front of her. Up close he looked like the word "wizened," although she wasn't exactly sure what that meant.

"You going to eat that stuff?" he asked, eyeing the opened box.

Penny rolled the candy around in her mouth, but didn't answer. Best not to talk to strangers on a bus.

"Here you go." He pulled the paper sack over his seat and dropped it onto her lap.

The engine rumbled to life, idling unevenly as Penny sat up and opened the sack. In it were a couple of tangerines and a box of Ritz crackers. And a pack of Lucky Strikes. Penny looked up at the old man. His eyes were like slits beneath his hat.

"Thought you were hungry. That's why you stole back there."

She dug further into the sack. There was a box of wooden matches, a black plastic comb, a bar of Lux soap, pistachios dyed red and two bottles of Fanta orange soda.

"I used to smoke cigarettes, too," he said, "and I know what's it's like to go without."

Penny fingered the Lucky Strikes. The old man laughed a raspy laugh, followed by a series of wheezings. The bus jerked and he went down into his seat. She held her breath, waiting for him to pop over the top again and ask if he could sit next to her and diddle her while they entered Oklahoma.

Penny waited. Quietly she pulled at the paper wrapping and carefully tore back the foil. She tapped out a cigarette, lighting it with the scrape and sizzle of a wooden match. Nothing. Not a peep from his seat. She blew a perfect smoke ring over the top of his head as the bus began to move over the gravel, rocking and braking toward the black highway.

Penny ate a cracker between drags on her cigarette. She was thirsty but didn't have a bottle opener, so she peeled off the loose skin of a tangerine with her teeth and pulled out a section, sucking on the tangy, sour fruit and spitting the seeds back into the sack.

The bus roared out onto the highway and began moving down the road, gaining speed as the store disappeared from sight. Telephone poles loped along the horizon. Disheveled houses passed swiftly by.

After a few miles, the suspense of waiting for the old man to reappear at her side—a blanket sheepishly covering his privates—got to Penny. She crawled onto her knees. She was going to give him back the sack and give him Al's camera and tell him they were square, in no uncertain terms.

Penny leaned aggressively over the back of his seat and was met with the top of a brown, balding head, nodding in sleep with the rise and fall of the road. Wisps of long, white hair curled around the old man's fuzzy ears and his bifocals had slipped to the very end of his pointed, brown nose. A little saliva shone on the corner of his mouth. He was covered with a nubby blue blanket scarred with cigarette holes. The *New York Times* crossword puzzle hung from his lap, mostly filled in. She sat back down and leaned her forehead against the back of the old man's seat.

"Don't talk to strangers on the bus, Penny!" Al had nagged, following Penny as she made her way along the bus depot.

"I know, I know, Al. I'm not stupid!" Penny took the hard bagel from him and mounted the steps onto the bus. Al ran up the platform alongside the bus. When he got to Penny's window, he stuck his fingers inside and pulled himself up on his toes.

"Listen to me." He shoved his face inside the bus. "I'm just saying, Penny," he whispered, peering around inside the bus, travelers jostling past him outside. "You don't know what people are like." His breath was like fire. "Maybe they will—" His voice broke.

"Christ, Al." Penny bit her lip. Al sunk down onto the platform and took a long draw from the bottle he carried inside a rumpled paper sack. Penny got onto her knees and leaned out the window.

"You know, Penny," Al called up from between the legs of people shoving by. "I been thinking."

"About?"

The bus driver revved the engine and Al had to shout. "Maybe I should head north, instead. Alaska. I could be a chef on a fishing boat. Whaddya think?"

Diesel exhaust fumed between them.

"But how—?" The bus began to pull away from the platform. The driver honked twice.

"Whaaa—?" Al cupped his hand to his ear. The bus swung around a corner and Al and the bus depot disappeared.

The old man had begun to snore. Penny sidestepped into the aisle, taking her things with her, and swayed up to the driver.

"What's the next stop?" she asked.

"Shamrock, Texas."

"Anything there?"

"Depends on what you want," he said, looking her up and down.

Penny turned back down the aisle. Suppose it does.

Penny came to the old man's side. She watched him nod and twitch in his sleep. She backed up a few steps and snapped his photo.

She pulled the bottles of orange Fanta from the sack and carefully set them down in the seat next to him, right next to his wallet and his ticket. She sat back down and lit a cigarette. There was one more exposure left in the camera. Maybe when the old man woke up she'd ask him to take her picture. Maybe they'd share the Fantas and he'd tell her where he came from, where he was going. *My name's Penelope,* she would tell him. *I have cousins in New York who love me.*

Penny thought about sending the photos back to Home On the Range with a note for Al: *Wish you were here. Please forward.* But the photographs, she knew, would probably be blurred. And underexposed. And one day, with any luck, she wouldn't even remember where she'd been.

Las Golondrinas

Oreos were her favorite snack, and she had a whole plate of them to herself, but Toby was inconsolable. Her mother was leaving. Again. Toby rubbed her nose and squeezed her eyes shut, trying not to cry. She knew crying would just fuel her mother's path out the door into the hot morning, away from her, away from Dad. Gone forever, every time. She broke her cookies into pieces.

Penelope was on the telephone, scheduling to be picked up in fifteen minutes. Ed pleaded softly, "Don't go, don't go." He pried Penelope's long fingers from the black receiver one by one. She dropped the phone and marched out of the kitchen.

Ed caught it and whispered into the receiver, "She's not going. Hello? She's cuh-cancelled. Can you hear me? She's made a muh-muh—a muh—" He tapped the hook several times while Toby watched, hopeful. She nodded her head in encouragement. "Tell them she's sorry, Dad."

An early June bug slipped into the kitchen through a tear in the bottom of the screen door and made buzzing swoops at Ed, who had finally given up on the call and was sitting quietly at the yellow formica table. Toby and Ed listened to Penelope zip and snap and drag her bags through the living room out onto the porch. When the front door opened and closed, Toby crawled into Ed's lap. He rested his sandpapery chin against her forehead. A moment later, a car pulled up, revved its engine, and Penelope's laughter joined with others. The car roared down the street, and the sound of Penelope faded into neighborhood noise: children shrieking at play, a dog barking, a lawn mower rattling next door.

Riding to school on her bike the next day, Toby passed California Bowl, not yet open at that hour but still busy with iridescent pigeons sashaying around the lot. Toby rode her bike across the asphalt and stopped at the entrance to the restaurant side of the building. At California Bowl, Penelope was a waitress. She wore big black shoes that she hated. Toby knew she hated them because every night after work, the shoes flew across the living room and slammed off the back door, making Petey, the dog, dive under the couch.

Toby rolled her bicycle back down to the sidewalk and tried to picture her mother happy, tried to picture Penelope smiling when she put a plate of food in front of strangers. Instead, Toby knew, her mother read colorful brochures about other places, brochures that piled up week after week, month after month until the day when Penelope would announce she was going away.

"She's gone for good this time, Dad, I can feel it." Toby had wept into Ed's shirt.

"She'll be back, Toby. She will."

But Toby knew differently. Toby saw the frown on Penelope's face when Ed cut coupons from the newspaper, trimming the edges of each one with little manicure scissors. Or when he came in from the garden that day having dug up the entire backyard in search of a buried bone for Petey. Or when he stuttered into the telephone, over and over again, patiently trying to get his point across.

What did her mother want? Toby could only guess, but she was sure it wasn't her father. Probably not Toby, either. Together Ed and Toby would sit in the booth closest to the bowling lanes, rapt at the efficient figure of Penelope, tall and neat, ready to serve. Toby shivered with admiration as her mother sweet-talked a cab driver into an extra order of onion rings for a bigger tip. Or when she'd manage to carry five plates of fries with gravy on them to the teenagers who were always singing and stuff, clapping and shouting, "Praise the Lord!" When Penelope would come to take their order, Toby and Ed would clutch each other's hands with delight. But Toby saw the distraction in her mother's eyes as Ed stammered out their order. Toby grinned maniacally and stroked her mother's hand to make up for Ed's failings. It was only a matter of time, Toby felt, when her mother would leave for good.

Toby knew they needed help. She dragged Ed to the guidance counselor at school.

"Tell her, Dad. Tell her it's not normal. Tell her it's awful."

Toby picked at a scab on her elbow while the counselor told them not to worry, Penelope just liked to take vacations. Ed chewed the nails on one hand, the one he used for the 10-key at Maxson Trucking, while he explained to the counselor that each time Penelope went away they worried that the charms of Ed's habits and Toby's quirks would fade a little more from Penelope's mind. Or that the almost painful satisfaction they shared at the taste of coarse salt on french fries, the blissful slurp of a malted, was not in any way shared by Penelope, who routinely, predictably, looked around at her life and said, "See ya."

The counselor didn't believe a word he said, Toby could tell by the way she eyed Ed's chaotic hair and the shiny worn spots of his corduroy pants.

"Thank you very much," Toby said with exaggerated decorum. "We'll be going now." To Ed she whispered, "C'mon, Dad. Let's get the hell out."

After school when Ed placed a dish of twisted-open Oreos in front of Toby, she held onto his thin wrist.

"She won't be back this time, Dad. You don't know. You don't know how much she *hates* us!"

Ed bent down and held Toby's face nose to nose with his. Toby looked straight into her father's eyes, brown like hers, and tried to telepathically turn him into Prince Charming.

Suddenly Ed stood up straight. "I have an idea." He pointed to the sky. "A good one."

"Oh no."

Toby followed Ed into her bedroom. He pulled a suitcase from the closet.

"Let's go." Ed tossed socks into the suitcase.

"Go where?"

"Get your stuff, Toby dear. We are leaving, too."

"But—?"

"It's okay, Tobes." He held a pair of underwear in one hand, a sneaker in the other. He smiled weakly. "Come with me, okay?"

Toby fished around under her bed for the stash of See's suckers Ed gave her when Penelope wasn't looking. She studied the shelf of souvenirs Penelope had given her after each return, and selected the ceramic kissing dolls. The dolls only kissed if they got close enough to each other. That and a sweater and she climbed into the old Rambler.

It usually took Ed three times around the approaching traffic circle before he could maneuver the car into the lane toward Pacific Coast Highway. Toby held her breath and braced herself. Ed gripped the steering wheel with both hands. He careered around the circle twice, then veered just in time out onto the highway.

"Good job, Dad."

Ed whistled nonchalantly.

The sky was a rich, bright blue along the ocean when the highway finally made its way to the beach. It was the same color as her mother's eyes, which grew navy and twinkly at dusk.

"I'm hungry," she told Ed, just as he slammed on the brakes. Toby fell to the floorboard. The car swerved right, then left, and Ed let out a whoop.

"What was it?" Toby asked, knowing her father had risked everything—even Toby—for a raven or possum or a lost dog. She climbed back onto the seat and looked out the back window.

"Cat. Poor little cat," Ed whispered, sadly shaking his head, and then, half-singing, "Lost its way. Looking for home, home, home." Toby settled back onto the seat. She held the kissing dolls on her lap and moved them slowly toward each other, their bobbing, dangling heads blindly heading toward each other. Her stomach flip-flopped when their lips pointed and the magnet took over, making them kiss.

She tried not to care where they were headed. It wouldn't help to ask her father since chances were slim he knew the way there, knew the direct route, the correct path. All asking would get Toby was a burning anxiety until they either arrived where he had planned or ended up someplace else.

After a while they pulled in at a roadside diner. Toby climbed onto a chrome and pink stool. A jukebox on the counter offered "Downtown," Penelope's favorite song. Toby didn't even have to ask, Ed was that way. He automatically fished a nickel out of his pocket. Toby swung her legs side to side, humming along with Petula Clark. She wanted her mother, and a greasy paper bag of french fries, and the flapping wings of the pigeons at California Bowl.

"What would you like, Tobarino? Have anything."

"I want Mom."

Ed nodded. "How 'bout a grilled cheese?"

"Okay."

A brunette waitress approached, smiling at Ed. She wore a white cap, and there was a little swatch of Kleenex sticking out of the low round collar of her pink uniform. She liked Ed right off the bat, Toby could tell by the way she leaned on the counter and rocked side to side. Penelope did that at work too, sometimes, and it made Toby nervous, because there would be poor old Dad watching Mom twitch and smile for someone else.

"No, that's all really. Two grilled cheese, two french fries, two colas. No coffee. No candy. No handy dandy."

The waitress laughed and nodded over to Toby.

"So where you goin', huh? Out for a ride with Pop?"

"I don't know. Ask him." Toby nodded toward her father, who had emptied the salt shaker onto the counter. "Mom left us."

Ed drew circles in the salt distractedly. The waitress abruptly straightened up.

"Sorry to hear that." She frowned at Ed. "Just where *are* you going, huh?"

They waited for Ed to look up from the pile of salt. Finally, Toby yelled, "Dad!"

Ed jerked his head up. "Who?"

"Where'ya taking the little girl, huh?" The waitress was peering intently at Ed.

"There's something I want Toby to see," Ed finally said, brushing the salt onto the floor.

The waitress looked at Toby, who shrugged. "Don't ask me," Toby said. "I only work here." Ed smiled. This was a Penelope joke, but the waitress seemed to get it, too. She left to turn in their order, and Toby sighed.

"Where?"

"Someplace special, Tobes. You'll see."

"Mexico?" Toby knew they were headed south. Mexico was the end of the line that way.

"Kind of."

"Kind of? What's 'kind of' like Mexico except Mexico?"

Toby was worried they weren't actually going anywhere, or even if there was a there to get to, her father wouldn't be able to find it. Like last week, when they were supposed to be going to her softball game but after twice bouncing over the meridian to head the opposite way, they still didn't make it to the game. Instead, they ended up at Lakewood Shopping Center circling the lot. Finally, Ed bought ice cream cones, one for her and one for Petey.

Petey had picked up Ed's confusions early on. All Toby had to do was whisper the word "sit" and Petey would take off at breakneck speed. He ran the perimeter of the backyard, kicking up great chunks of Ed's garden. Ed ran after the dog, yelling, "Sit, Petey! Sit!," which only made Petey run faster.

The waitress walked by smiling again. Toby resisted the urge to reach out and grab her hand and beg her to point them in the right direction.

They drove down Highway 1. After an hour or so, Ed pulled off the road at a little wooden shack painted yellow. He bought a bag of red pistachios and dried apricots for dinner, and ordered a date shake, which they divided into two tall cups. For miles, Ed and Toby happily slurped the thick sweet liquid through paper straws. Eventually they passed a sign that read San Clemente. Ed cruised by several motels, then chose one right on the beach. Toby waited patiently while the clerk asked Ed to repeat himself three times. Finally they got a key and went to their room.

Ed turned the television to Ted Mack's *Amateur Hour* and Toby fell asleep to the swish swish of low tide, the heavy smell of night-blooming jasmine.

In the morning, Ed stood at Toby's bedside as she awakened. He handed her a red bathing suit. He wore green trunks. Toby held his hand as they walked along the silky dark sand, stopping to pick up a piebald shell.

"What is it?"

"I think it's a scallop. See how it's scuh-scuh-scuh... ridged?" Ed ran his long fingers around the wavy edge of the shell.

"I want to keep it," Toby said. "I'll save it for Mom. In case she ever comes back."

Ed held the shell, and then the next and the next. He cupped the shells stiffly, as if holding a bowl of holy water.

Toby stuck her toes into the sand and was frightened when the water rushed up to her feet, surrounding them and sucking the sand out from under her. She sank further and further. Ed stood sinking, too, smiling encouragement, lifting the shells in an attempt at waving.

Toby splashed around in the salty, foaming water until she was scratchy with sand and hungry. They went back to the room, showered, then walked down the street to have breakfast, passing outcroppings of swaying pampas grass. They found a small café, Las Olas.

Toby ate chorizo scrambled into eggs and soft corn tortillas. An ocean breeze swirled through the open doors of the restaurant. Toby's nose and cheeks were hot and burnt, and her skin felt soft as the sound of the waves.

By the time they finished breakfast, the California sun had traveled high into the sky and the car was broiling inside.

Ed turned on the fan and steered them off El Camino Real up Camino Capistrano, inland, away from the beach.

"Where do you think she is?" Toby asked.

"I don't know, Toby. Somewhere." He yanked his earlobe twice.

"Somewhere pretty, like here?"

"I don't know. I'm sorry."

Toby turned the radio on to distract her father and herself. What good would it do to think about her mother, where she might be? There were no answers. Toby made Ed laugh by singing "Wild Thing" along with the radio.

They pulled into an asphalt parking lot in the midst of a whorl of narrow streets. Ed led Toby up the sidewalk along a low clay wall painted white, brilliant in the hot sun. The sidewalk led to a brick arch. There was a wooden cross on top of the arch.

"Are we here?" Toby asked.

"Yes, in we go!" and they passed through a turnstile.

"Two, please," Ed said into a window cut into the thick white wall. Toby read a sign: BIENVENIDOS. WELCOME TO MISSION SAN JUAN CAPISTRANO.

Toby felt as if she had walked onto another planet. The dirt beneath her sandals was pink and beige and sticky. A salamander, apricot but fading, ran by Toby's feet. She followed the tiny quick animal out into the sunlight, around a corner onto an open plaza, sand covered and undulant with crumbling walls, little paper flags marking significant sites, like candle forms and brick-making ovens.

She looked around and spotted Ed sniffing candy-colored flowers dangling from baskets hung along a redbrick wall.

"Look at the hummingbirds, dear. And fuchsia. They love the fuchsia."

Together they walked around the plaza, reading wooden plaques describing artifacts. There was a huge stone wheel, "used for crushing olives for cooking oil," Ed read from a booklet.

"The walls are adobe, Toby. Adobe Toby. Toby adobe—"

"Okay, Dad. Got it."

They strolled along paths shaded by the lacy branches of pepper trees. Ed stopped to finger the crook of a eucalyptus tree whose bark resembled skin, wrinkled and soft in the joints, flesh-colored and smooth along the limbs.

"Listen to this, Toby," Ed called out, bringing Toby back from plucking a lush gardenia she had buried her nose in.

He read from the pamphlet as if performing on stage: " 'The corridors you walk have known the soft footsteps of dark-eyed Indians and brown-robed Franciscans.' "

"What's a Franciscan?"

"Um—someone who likes to live alone, I think. Yes. That's it." He turned a page. "Let's look at the chapel."

They wandered along the cool corridors. The afternoon sun was no match for the thick adobe walls, the terra cotta shingles. A complex threshold of twisted vines of coral and salmon and mother-of-pearl bougainvillea shaded the walkways. Honeysuckle and wisteria dripped sweet blossoms onto the brick paths.

When they entered the dark interior of the church, Toby was alarmed.

"Is something on fire?"

"No-no-no-no. It's incense, Toby, it's the Holy Ghost. It's angels."

Thin spires of white smoke twirled upward to join in a thick cloud filling the small room. Toby watched Ed inhale deeply, his eyes closed, a faint smile spreading across his face.

She slipped beneath the pew onto the stone floor. The smooth, cold hardness of the stone was solid and comforting. She thought about the bare feet of the Indian mothers, fat babies seeking crumbs.

Ed bent down and peered at Toby. Then he lay down on his back and shuffled his body until they were shoulder to shoulder beneath the pew, his long legs sticking out into the aisle.

"I remember your mother," Ed said, and Toby thought miserably that she had been right all along. Her mother was gone for good.

"She was so angry with me. I had gotten lost, you know." Ed ran his thin index finger along the seam of the wood above their heads. "By the time we got off the highway it was a hundred degrees. No shade anywhere. And then the next morning I made her get up at dawn to see them coming."

"See who? Are we meeting someone here?" Suddenly Toby felt a rush of hope. "Is it Mom? Is this where she is, Dad?"

"No, Toby." Ed maneuvered out from under the pew and stood up. His voice echoed above her. "She's not here...I don't think."

Suddenly Toby wanted to grab her father's ankle and shake and shake and shake him. Of course she wasn't here! She balled up her fists and pounded on the pew over her head.

"Where is she where is she where is she!" she shouted. "Where is my *mother*!"

"Toby, stop. Shush." Ed grabbed at Toby under the pew, but she sidled out the other side. She ran out of the church. As she headed for the sunlight she heard Ed yell, "You look just like your mother when you're mad!"

Toby walked disconsolately around the mission, trying to avoid her father, who seemed bent on following her, reading aloud from the booklet just as if she were by his side. She hated herself and her mother and even her father. Why did he have to be so ... so ...? Toby couldn't put her finger on what it was about her father, but there had to be something. There had to be some reason her mother left them over and over again. Or maybe it was just Toby. Her own selfish needs and whining and tears all the time.

Of course Mom had left. Why not? Mom was a circle of black shiny hair and eyes filled with the sky, not the worrisome, awkward weight of Toby and Ed, stumbling along in life.

"Your eyes are the ocean," Toby would say, and her mother would say, "Yours are fields of wheat and the sun," and Toby would stroke Penelope's long hair, just the way Ed would while absentmindedly working a jigsaw puzzle.

"Poor old Dad," Toby sighed, then walked back to Ed, who was mid-paragraph.

" 'The legend of the swallows is the favorite of them all.' "

Ed rested his hand on Toby's head for a moment. "Let's look at the cactus." He steered them out into the sunshine, to an enormous collection of cacti—some tall and thin and blooming one large pink flower, others round as pincushions, others tiny, like trees in a desert for gnomes.

" 'When the March sun is warm—' "

"Like today?"

"Yes, Toby. 'When the March sun is warm and the orange trees are heavy with sweet white blossoms—"

"I smelled them out in the backyard!"

"Okay, Tobettes." Ed continued: " 'If you should say, what a beautiful spring day it is, the reply from *los viejos*'—that means old-timers, it says here—'the reply would be *sí*, a beautiful day, but when *las golondrinas* come back, then it will be spring.' "

"Say it again?"

"*Las golondrinas*. That means the swallows."

Toby wandered back to the chapel to cool off while Ed settled onto a bench with his reading materials.

She noticed a shallow door on the right side of the chapel. She pushed it open and stepped into a tiny, smoke-filled room, hundreds of candles burning in small jars. The incense and smoke made her cough. Through the white smoke she made out a figure, a man it seemed, standing or kneeling on a table. Toby came closer and suddenly saw it was a statue of a man pointing to his own leg, a bloody gash stripping away the flesh. Toby backed away, trying not to cry out. She bumped into Ed and wrapped her arms around him, burying her face in his stomach. Ed took her hand and led her outside.

"Your mother always says those saints aren't good for children to see."

"I'm tired, Dad. Let's go home, okay?"

"We will, dear Toby, as soon as the swallows settle back in."

Ed and Toby wandered all through the mission until finally dusk began to fall. They sat on a stone bench in the plaza. Several other people stood with their heads tilted back, gazing at the sky. Ed placed a nickel in Toby's palm and she bought a pile of peanuts from a metal dispenser. She threw the nuts, and pigeons swirled and landed. Toby sat next to her father.

Ed watched the sky. "Penelope thought we were lost. Then she thought I was crazy."

"When?"

"Before you were born. Before."

"Not like now, huh?"

Ed laughed. "Well, we are always a little lost, huh Tobe? Always a little off, but—"

Something zoomed in front of them, swift and small. Then three more. Tiny birds—Toby counted ten, then fifteen, then lost count—zigzagged, hovered, soared, and then disappeared under the eaves of the mission. The people standing around applauded.

"What are they, Dad? The swallows?"

Ed nodded his head, his eyes closed and arms outstretched. "I can smell your mother's perfume." He breathed deeply.

Toby picked up the booklet and read: "'Like strings of rosary beads, their gourd-like nests cling to the eaves of the limestone arches of the great stone church.'"

"I can still hear her gasp when the birds came. It was dawn and so lovely and cool." Toby noticed for the first time that Ed's shirt was buttoned wrong. "She didn't believe me when I told her. Penny, darling, I said, it's magic. It's God. They come back exactly on March 19th."

"It's March 20th," Toby said.

"Is it? Huh. It was then, too. What a co-co-. What a co—"

"Coincidence?"

"Don't you think?"

"I guess so. I mean, how should I know?"

"You're right, Toby. Sorry."

Ed parallel parked the Rambler by a restaurant called Las Golondrinas, on a short street a few blocks from the mission. They took a table outside on a patio overlooking a railroad. Impatiens hung from the terra cotta roof and night-blooming jasmine was everywhere.

"The Atchison, Topeka, and the Santa Fe," Ed sang, while Toby studied the darkening sky, navy and glimmering with stars. Ed ordered, stammering out Spanish words. Within a few minutes the waitress brought them crunchy folded tortillas filled with pieces of white fish and cilantro and tomatoes. Ed sprinkled a crushed lime onto half an avocado. On Toby's placemat was a drawing of the little birds.

"Where do they go, Dad?"

"*Las golondrinas*? I don't know, Toby. I suppose I could look it up." Ed wiped salsa from his mouth. "They always come back, though." He took a large bite out of his taco.

"On March 20th?"

"Legend says March 19th." Ed scrunched up his shoulders. "Sometimes things get a little off. A little off, right?"

Toby sipped her almond-flavored drink and watched her father lick each finger carefully, one by one.

They drove back the long way, as Ed explained when Toby asked why they were not back on El Camino Real.

"I'll bet it's the long way," Toby mumbled, knowing it could be two nights before they reached home.

"This road's better, Tobe, you'll see."

Toby peered out into the pitch-black night. It would be two nights and her mother would have come and gone again, and the dog would be starved to death, lying out in that ditch in the backyard. After a while it began to rain. Ed slowly pulled the Rambler to the side of the road.

"What are we doing, Dad?" Toby had dozed off and was dreaming that a salamander was chewing on her toes. She rolled down the window and a rush of fresh wet wind blew into the car.

Ed got out and leaned against the car.

"What do you smell, Toby?"

"Dad...Dad, *please* get back into the car."

"Horses?"

Ed's eyes were closed, his hands in his pockets, raindrops splattering his hair and face. "I smell horses and mustard. And sage, smell that, Tobes?" Ed began to walk down the road ahead of them, his eyes still closed. He listed to the left. Toby got out of the car.

"Daa-aa-d! I want to go home!" She was cold and wet. And her father was leaving.

Ed halted. "Listen! Hear that? It's an owl, Toby. A bird of the night."

Toby listened to a soft crashing sound, and then the reedy hooting of an owl. She shivered. Ed walked further away, disappearing into the darkness at the end of the light from the headlamps.

Toby climbed back into the car and slammed the door. "Just go! *Go on!* I don't care!" Then she yelled, "*I don't care!*" She got to her knees and pumped the horn with all her might. "I don't care—I don't care—I don't *care!*"

Ed reemerged from the shadows. He crawled into the car and pulled the door shut. He wiped the water from his face and took Toby's hand. "I'm so sorry, Toby. So so sorry." He was crying.

Toby held her father's cold, wet hand. She looked out into the night, into the chaparral and moonlit hills and thought about how round the earth was, how birds swirled around it to some unseen force. She imagined the force coming from somewhere inside of her, pulling her from the car. She would leap away from the car and her father and swoop up the road, up into the treetops. She'd stay there all through the night. In the morning she would take a long trip to someplace pretty and warm, and when she grew tired, she'd find the cool shade of a sacred eave. And she wouldn't come back. Ever.

Egg Heaven

The windows of Egg Heaven—painted with dancing eggs—were already steamed up by eight in the morning when Vince limped to his regular place: the booth by the kitchen. He placed his wooden cane next to him, a barrier against idle conversation that had worked well every day since he'd returned from Nam, ten years ago.

At the counter, Clara fluttered her fingers at Vince and slipped slices of bread into the tin toaster carousel. Minutes later she swabbed the pieces that slid out onto the tray with a brush dipped in oil. For Vince, she salted the lightly toasted bread.

Vince spotted Angel, the cook, through the kitchen doorway. The men waved to each other.

"The usual?" Angel winked at Vince.

It didn't seem possible to Vince that he was capable of eating the same thing every day, but Angel's Special—sunny-side-up eggs on greasy hash browns with a dash of Tabasco—was exactly what Vince craved every morning. That, and the routine of toast, Clara, coffee, his work.

Placing his weight onto his cane, Vince rose and poured himself a cup of coffee, the privilege of being a regular, an animate object in the still life of Egg Heaven. The chipped off-white cups were so tiny Vince finished his first in three gulps, then refilled it.

He eased himself back into the booth. Angel brought the steaming plate of potatoes and eggs to him.

"Good morning, my friend." Angel gestured toward Vince's sketchbook. "Same thing today?"

Vince nodded.

Angel rubbed his graying beard thoughtfully. "Good luck." He flung a white towel over his shoulder and went back to the kitchen.

Clara brought his toast. "Will you show me something today?"

He wanted to. Wanted to open up his sketchbook and say, look, here, Clara, what do you see? And he wanted to know why she had asked him to walk home with her the day before. She'd filled the last coffeepot with salt and ice, shaken it hard, then set it down and looked at Vince's cane. "Walk me home?" That's all she'd said.

Vince had trailed behind Clara as she walked to her apartment. He was saddened by the smallness of the buildings, a set of raggedy one-story apartments built for single people. Single like Clara, Vince prayed, Clara with the straight lemon-colored hair hanging heavily down the back of her bluejean jumper. He had walked her home after her shift at Egg Heaven, not knowing why or how it had happened. He leaned on his cane, waiting for Clara to turn and say goodbye. A bush tangled around a low wrought-iron gate, and Vince traced the shape of a thorn, waiting.

But she was fumbling with the door, so Vince stepped up to help. Clara pulled a yellow sheet of paper from the screen door. It was smudged with blue ink. Grimy tape held a check to the paper.

"This check is bad. You are evicted. Be out in two days."

Clara stuffed the notice into her pocket. Vince felt the hot blush rise in her cheeks before he saw it, wanted to say something appropriate, but what would that be? He had no idea. He'd lost track of such things. Besides, Clara quickly shoved the key into the lock, said, "Bye," and disappeared into the dark.

"Can I see?"

Vince shrugged and looked at his hands. "They're not ready." The bell over the door rang as new customers came in, and Clara went back to her work.

Vince scooped the food into his mouth in rushed forkfuls, wanting to get back to work, then pushed his plate away. He opened a tissue paper packet of charcoal and the sketchbook and began to draw Clara's face.

He knew so little about her. She'd come to Egg Heaven a couple of years before. At first, Vince had hardly noticed her, quiet as she was. His mornings often seemed so loud, especially after sleepless nights filled with memories, that the gray-eyed waitress with long blonde hair was like a passing illusion, a flutter of warmth hovering above his cold, aching body. But time passed, and gradually Clara came into focus. She was about his age, maybe thirty. Quiet and tired, she seemed. And always distracted. Vince had caught her many times suddenly frozen in place, concern clouding her eyes. Or oddly bent, methodically rubbing her smooth ankle. He had begun to draw her then.

This morning, he drew Clara as she listened to a customer complain, wiping her red hands round and round a damp cloth. She had dark creases under her eyes. He thought about the eviction notice, his glimpse of the dark interior before she closed her door. He thought he could make out twin beds, a squat refrigerator, a small TV. And a large dark piece of furniture, maybe a piano. It seemed to fill the small room.

Later, when she came over to his table with her own cup of coffee, he closed his sketchbook. Clara sat in the booth with him and began to add up the customers' bills. When Vince asked about the apartment, Clara rested her chin in her hands. In his mind, Vince traced the line of her long fingers down one side of her face, then the other.

"I have to be out by tomorrow."

She said "I," not "we," and Vince felt himself flush. It wasn't that he couldn't just ask, Clara, are you alone, too? But somehow—even though he never saw her with anyone else—he felt the answer would be no, she's not alone, and then what would he do? He would be left to imagine Clara with a circle of warm bodies moving in orbit around her, Clara like a winter sun, so far away.

"I have to figure something out." She gathered up the bills and went back to the counter.

He quickly turned back to his drawing. The image of the reddish knuckles and delicate crosshatch patterns across Clara's hands quickened his heart, and he chose a stick of burnt sienna charcoal.

By three o'clock, Vince had worked on ten drawings and shook from caffeine. He stood to stretch and leave, spying Clara outside on the bus bench, looking up into the sky.

Angel came out from the kitchen, a jangle of keys on his hip. He poured one last cup of coffee for Vince and himself, then rinsed the empty glass pot.

Angel gestured to the sketchbook. "Let me see, okay?" Angel turned the pages of the day's drawings. Every once in a while, he looked up at Vince, his moustache curling around the ends of his smile, the crow's feet at the corners of his eyes curving down. Vince loved Angel's round face, the almost imperceptible ghost of light in his eyes.

"This one," Angel said, turning the book toward Vince, opened to the sketch of Clara's hands around her face. "Show her this one."

"No. It's not ready."

"But it is beautiful!" Angel placed his hand on Vince's chest. "Show her, *amigo*."

"Thanks, Angel." Vince pronounced it An-hel, the soft *g* so fitting for his gentle friend. "Maybe soon."

For months Vince sketched parts of Clara. On bad days, days when what he saw in Nam played over and over again in his head, days when he couldn't even roll out of bed, Vince left off his Clara drawings and with a leaky fountain pen drew thick lines so tightly woven nothing but a black smear would be left. Sometimes he turned the smear into an eye, and sometimes he tried to close the eye, but he couldn't accomplish even that small task because fear made his palms wet with sweat, and weak.

Those were the worst days, alone in the blue clapboard house that he shared with no one. No one home when he came back from Vietnam. His mother had died. His girlfriend had followed her new lover to Canada. He felt so undone by what he had seen that he couldn't bring himself to respond to his Nam-buddy Pablo's many phone calls.

What he saw, what he saw, the girl's tear-streaked face as the guys pushed her back into the hut, her scream, Vince moving as if underwater toward her. Then there had been an explosion. Shrapnel like lightning slivered his right thigh, sending him to his left knee, then face down into the water. Pablo rolled him over. "Let's go!" he yelled, dragging Vince through the maelstrom. When water ran clear from his eyes, Vince saw the girl's hand in a tree. Severed, graceful and limp, it draped across a green shoot, blood like sap slipping slowly along the leaves.

Vince was sent home, one long piece missing from his thigh. He used a cane the doctors said he didn't need.

But he did. He limped around the old house day after day, dusting rooms so empty even his breath echoed. Nam was a long time ago, years ago, but there were still nights when the images bent him over, making him draw. Some days he threw each picture away with ritual grace—launching them across the room like so many doomed paper airplanes.

He did not throw Clara away, though. Her unfinished gaze, half of the triangle of her chin, the space around two lines of her neck, he could not throw these away though they broke him open with longing so great he cried for drugs he did not possess, for drugs he had sworn to fight off hand to hand, whatever it took. Now all he faced was the interminable hobbling up Ximeno to Fourth Street each day, just a thread from dissolution. Sometimes when the thread threatened to break, a bus would roar by and turn the world into gagging fumes and firebombs. And when the noise stopped and he could breathe again, feel again, he would realize it had been only a city bus and he would be, miraculously, at the top of the hill—at Egg Heaven—simply waiting for the light to change from red to green.

Vince was unsettled as he sketched. He hadn't slept for a whole week, thinking impossible thoughts. When Clara sat down with her coffee, Vince tried to form the words he wanted to speak, the plan he'd imagined would work. But Clara spoke first.

"I'm living upstairs." She did not look at Vince.

"At Angel's?" Vince felt his chest contract and he scratched at it.

"Yes." She seemed embarrassed.

Vince fingered the rough edges of the new key in his pocket. It was silly, of course. It was an absurd idea, the worst one yet, Vince thought, and gathered up his things. Clara went back to her customers.

Vince limped out of the restaurant and around to the back and peeked his head into the kitchen. "Angel!" he hissed.

"*Sí?*" Angel whirled around.

"She's living with you?"

Angel sighed. "It is temporary, *mi amigo*. She had no place to go."

Vince stared at the cement floor, leaned heavily on his cane, breathing hard.

"*Amigo*, please," Angel began, but Vince turned and banged awkwardly out the door.

It was only one o'clock. Too many hours until he could allow himself to get into bed, turn on the television, wrap himself in sheets worn by his compulsive laundering. Vince looked up and down Fourth Street, the liquor store such an easy walk, the honeysuckle swarming with bees next to the doorway that led up to Angel's apartment.

Vince stood for long minutes outside Egg Heaven, listening to Angel plunge a mop into a pail, drag chairs around the cement floor. He scratched at the dull ache in his chest. When Angel finally came out, he seemed surprised to see Vince still there.

"It is temporary, for sure." Angel stretched his long brown arms to the sky, then rested his clasped hands on top of his head. He smiled. "Let me tell you something." He gestured Vince over to the bus bench and they sat together. "She was okay until her sister died. Now she's just another *loca* waitress. I've known too many of them, for sure."

The heat from the sun-streaked bus bench warmed Vince's aching thigh as he watched Angel's profile, his round nose, bronze skin, salt-and-pepper hair.

A sister, he thought. Clara had a sister. And now she's alone.

"They were twins," Angel said. "I don't think they had any other family. So she's all alone now. Like you, my friend." He turned to face Vince. "You know, *amigo*, you should not be so afraid of her." He laughed. "She is a strange one. Like you."

Vince and Angel sat silently in the sun for a while longer. "She cries all night." Angel patted Vince on the shoulder. "You should be with her, you know? You are getting old. Older, I mean."

Vince considered Angel his friend, though they had in common only the day-to-day routine of Egg Heaven: flipping the sign to ABIERTO, drinking cup after cup of coffee, changing the sign to CERRADO. But didn't that count? Vince had lost track of what counted as friendship. Or love.

The next morning, Vince was the only customer for more than an hour. Angel had gone back upstairs. Clara gazed out the window between the painted eggs. She had forgotten to turn on the radio, and the only sound was the toaster ferrying slices of bread, a pulsing growl. Vince was alarmed when Clara started to cry. He pulled paper napkins from the metal dispenser on the counter and handed them to her. "What's wrong?"

She just stood there, tears running down her cheeks, staring at him.

Finally, she blew her nose. "I'm so stupid, Vince. I screwed up." She came around the counter and sat down next to him. "It's the piano." She blew her nose and Vince noted the raw edges of her nostrils, the graceful way her head bent into the napkins.

"Your piano?"

"Our...yes, my piano. I left it in the apartment. Couldn't figure out how to take it with me. I don't have any money. It's probably gone now, probably someone's stolen it." Again she bent her head and tears seemed to splash down on her lap.

"Your piano? Clara, people don't generally steal pianos. I mean, they're so big and heavy."

She looked up, hesitant. Vince resisted the laugh of relief that gurgled up his throat. Just a piano? He could take care of that. "Let's just go get it and bring it back to Angel's."

"How, Vince? I don't have any money for movers. It's probably gone, anyway. It was my sister's piano. And I just left it there."

Vince imagined two Claras seated at a piano, children with blonde heads rocking side to side in unison, their little feet kicking in time to the music.

"Clara, listen to me. We'll just go get the piano. Right now."

She wiped her nose again. "How, Vince? It's not possible."

It had been so long since he'd called up his friends. Friendship didn't seem to be something Vince was cut out for anymore, since the war, since his injury, since the long quiet days of sketching and Egg Heaven.

But here was Clara, and she needed him. Finally.

"I'll call up my buddies. One of them has a truck. We'll just go get the piano, bring it back here."

"You're just saying that, Vince. You don't have any buddies. I know. I see you every day." Clara had stopped crying and now seemed exhausted, those dark creases reappearing under her eyes. "You don't have any buddies. I don't have my piano. I don't have—"

"Clara, trust me." Vince went to the pay phone in the threshold of the kitchen. He strained for long moments trying to remember Pablo's number. He slipped a dime in the slot and dialed. He watched Clara watching him from the counter.

A moment later Pablo was on the line. After a brief and vague explanation of why he hadn't called in so long—Mom's dead, stuff like that—Pablo said he still had the truck. Sure he'd help out. Today was fine. Vince thought about the steep stairs.

"There're stairs," he said.

"Yeah, man, there always are." Pablo told Vince he'd ring up the old crowd. Vince gave him the pay phone number and hung up.

Vince and Clara sat quietly sipping coffee, waiting for the phone to ring. Vince twisted a napkin around his finger, praying Pablo would come through for him. He wished he had his sketchbook. It was so rare that Clara was just sitting, almost like a model, so still. He wanted to ask her about the piano, about the sister, about where her heart was most of the time. Instead he sat twirling the napkin, waiting.

Fifteen minutes later the phone rang, and Vince jumped to answer it. Pablo and three other friends would be there in a few minutes. Vince smiled at Clara, who was walking toward him. By the time he hung up, Clara was standing close to him. The scent of her skin rose from the loose collar of her shirt and Vince felt his breathing slow, his legs weaken.

"Are they coming?" Clara gazed up at him.

"Yes. Right away." He wanted to touch his finger to her cheek, rub away the dark circles. He imagined choosing burnt sienna for the edges of her eyelids. Clara smiled.

"Here, sit down," she said, offering her arm. He had left the cane back at the counter, and now he shook—from his leg, her proximity. Soon old friends would be outside, waving and making him laugh again. He had fifteen minutes to prepare, but all he could do was rub his thigh.

When the truck pulled up, Clara ran out to meet them. Her hands fluttered in description of where the apartment was, and then Pablo—only a bit older than Vince remembered—came into Egg Heaven.

"Don't get up, man," Pablo said, putting a warm hand on Vince's shoulder. Vince peered up into his old friend's face, fleshed out a bit, a few lines crinkling from his eyes, but yes, it was Pablo. Vince took Pablo's other hand in both of his and pressed hard. His throat ached so much he couldn't speak.

"It's okay, Vince. We'll be back in a bit."

Pablo helped Clara into the cab. Clara waved at Egg Heaven, squinting through the windows to find Vince. Vince waved his cane, and the truck roared away.

After resting for a few moments, trying not to think about Clara's lithe body stepping into the truck, Vince went out the back door of the restaurant and climbed the dark stairwell to Angel's apartment. Several minutes passed before a young man opened the door. When he smiled, Vince could see he was related to Angel, with the same deep lines around his mouth, the same light in the eyes.

"Come in," he said, yelling "Angel!" into the apartment.

"*Gracias.*" Vince's thigh ached from the climb up the stairs. He lowered himself onto a low sofa that filled one wall of the living room. Angel came down the hall.

"*Amigo! Qué pasa?*" Angel looked concerned. Vince had never come up to the apartment before, although Angel had invited him many times to play cards, watch TV. Angel sat next to Vince on the sofa.

"Angel, I have something to tell you, I'm not sure you're going to like it."

"What?"

"Clara has a piano."

"*Sí*, so?"

"Well, it's coming here."

"Here?" Angel looked around. "Where?" And then he began to laugh. "Ha ha ha! *Sí*, a piano. Sure thing! Bring it in! Okay, come on!" Angel got up and went down the hallway. Vince heard him say something in Spanish, then another voice and another began to laugh heartily. Angel came back into the room, shaking his head, grinning. "*Loca güerita*," he said. Crazy white girl.

After the piano arrived, Vince hugged Pablo and shook hands with his old friends. The apartment had just stood empty, they said, except for the piano sitting there, waiting. Vince thanked them, promised to call Pablo soon. Angel and his cousins moved all the furniture around in the living room and pushed the piano against one wall.

Angel and Vince sat on the couch, Vince's cane propped against the mahogany spinet with its ornate lid. Clara flushed when Angel asked her to play, but she agreed and then dug through the piano bench, flipping through sheaves of music and books. Vince could tell—knowing her face so well, knowing the slant of fatigue and sorrow that often appeared when she was determined—Vince could tell she was alone in some tumultuous place that existed only in her memory.

Clara pulled out the bench, sat slightly to the left, and opened the book of music. Angel smiled at Vince. He seemed amused by this turn of events—first the *güerita*, then the piano, now the performance. Vince loved Angel at that moment, the moment right before Clara lifted her hands and placed them on the keyboard.

While she played, Vince imagined his light gray charcoal stick swiftly moving down one side of the page, outlining Clara's hips, her waist, the darker shade where her arms bent, where her fingers cast shadows across the keys.

But something was wrong with the music she was playing. It was not unappealing, but it was so low, so lacking in high notes. Vince didn't know much about music, but he could tell. Something was missing. He worried that the keys were broken, that something had been damaged in the move.

He rose and limped quietly to the piano, not wanting to disturb Clara's focus. Then he saw the sheet music. The top of the page read, *One piano, four hands.*

His heart hurt then, and as he watched, he noticed the pauses, saw how Clara heard what he did not, how her fingers hesitated, then responded to a sound that wasn't there. Not in the way she needed it to be. She played her part like the one leaf in a bush that shivers in the wind when all the others are still.

Clara's birthday was coming up. Vince had spied Angel wrapping a Spanish dictionary in butcher paper. Angel said her birthday was in three weeks.

Each morning for the next three weeks Vince stayed home and made instant coffee and drew Clara. Clara was in mourning, and Vince knew what that felt like. Mourning demanded obedience, silence, and the terrible hungry presence of the body. Vince was determined to trace the grief that lay just below the surface of her soft skin, square shoulders, delicate breasts, thin legs. It was the only way, he knew—he hoped—the only way to become whole again. For both of them.

Vince kept at his task the whole time, moving from the siennas and umbers and blacks to reds and pinks, then even a blue that matched the California sky. In between bouts of drawing, he cleaned his house. He slept fitfully. Finally, after the soreness left his hands and the stack of sketches was thick and smelling of his sweat, he took a warm shower. He thought how warm water was the same everywhere, how tears always tasted the same, whether they were his or someone else's.

He waited until the morning after Clara's birthday, to catch her alone. He'd found a perfect tiny box in his mother's old bureau that he kept in the hallway. He spent three hours painting the box with reds and yellows and greens. When it was dry, he put the extra key to his house in it, gathered the sketches into a sheaf, and went outside for the first time in weeks.

At the corner of Broadway and Ximeno, Vince stood for a moment at the intersection. Dawn was his favorite time, the time when the ocean breeze and keening gulls made him feel happy. Alive. Dawn in Long Beach was the safe time, when early risers, innocent and puffy faced, scuffed bougainvillea leaves and fuchsia buds from the sidewalk on their way to get the morning paper and a cup of coffee.

Vince waited at the door of Egg Heaven for Clara to come and open up the café. He peered through the window, between the painted eggs. Streamers announcing HAPPY BIRTHDAY hung from the walls. Balloons sagged from the counter near a pink half-eaten cake.

Vince heard the back door open and close as Clara entered Egg Heaven. She flipped on the lights and scanned the mess. She covered her face briefly with her hands. Then she noticed Vince outside, and rushed toward the door.

"Where have you been?" She opened the door for him. Vince followed Clara into Egg Heaven. Clara went straight to the coffeemaker.

"I've been busy." He lowered himself into the booth shakily. He had forgotten his cane. Clara filled two small cups from the dripping machine. She brought them to the booth and sat down across from Vince, who eyed the opened presents on the table: a calendar from the Wonder Bread Company, a drooping fern in a purple pot, a box of handkerchiefs.

"It was our—my birthday," Clara said, reddening slightly.

"I have a gift for you, too." He pushed the sheaf of sketches over to Clara. She looked at him, puzzled. "Go ahead. It's what I've been working on."

The sketchbook was wrapped with a heavy blue sheet of rough paper. When Clara opened it, she gasped.

"Sara!"

"What?" Vince asked. When Clara did not respond, he gently lifted her limp hand off the page. "There's more, look."

He turned page after page of his Clara sketches, remarking on some of them, not noticing that Clara was beginning to cry until one fat teardrop landed on the corner of a sketch. He looked up, startled.

"Clara, Clara." He dabbed at her cheeks with a paper napkin. His stomach rolled in sickening waves. Was it the drawings? No, Vince decided. No, because he had worked on them with everything in him, and he prayed, he *knew*, they were complete. Alive. There was wholeness in his Clara drawings, life on the verge of being lived. The moment had arrived: he pulled Clara toward him, murmuring, "Please don't cry." He touched her hair. In the blink of an eye, Clara slumped against him. Vince cradled her, trying to wrap her in his entire self. Was it possible for a human being to have hair this sweet, this soft? How could he have forgotten this, and the heat that rose from a human head, and the weight of it against him?

Clara reached a protective hand to the sketchbook.

"I have something else," he said. Still holding Clara tightly, he pulled the tiny box from his pocket.

She ran her fingers over the bright paint. "Pretty." Then she opened it.

Vince watched Clara carefully, the face he knew so well, the contours, the creases near her ears, the gray soft eyes burning red. And now the temperature of her, of Clara, the wetness and life beneath the surface.

Clara turned the key over and over in her palm. Then she touched the portrait staring up at her. "This looks just like Sara," she said. "My sister. She died."

Vince nodded. The sadness around Clara's mouth, along her fine neck and straight shoulders made him want to weep.

"We were twins. She—" Clara gazed out the window. "We were walking down Ocean Boulevard and she was mad at me as usual so I was walking behind her, you know, dragging my feet."

Vince held his breath. He knew this part, the recitation of events, the report of exactly what happened, and then the silence. He was ready.

"We had a fight that morning. I'd made breakfast and Sara scolded me about the eggs. She said, 'Why do you always break the yolk?'"

Vince couldn't help but smile at this. He held Clara around the shoulders, felt the bones and flesh, the scent of grief, the absent sister.

"I said, 'I don't *always*,' and she said, 'Yes, you do. They're a mess.' Then she got mad at me for always screwing up the second movement of a Schumann piece we were working on. We were supposed to give a recital, and I—I don't know, I got distracted or something. Anyway. She was right. The eggs were a mess."

Clara moved out from under Vince's arms. Vince relinquished her, silently praying, *Don't go.* She pulled her legs up beneath her on the booth, and began the habitual rubbing of her ankle.

Clara's leg bumped into Vince's under the table. Then Vince realized it was against him, warm, still. Clara slowly turned the pages of sketches, stopping at the one in profile. She ran her finger down the side of the face. "If I hadn't been ten steps behind her," she cleared her throat, swallowing hard, "it would have been both of us. Oh god, I miss her so much!"

Vince caught her hand. "Clara. I want you to come live with me." He said it in a rush. He didn't know what else to say. It isn't far? It's clean? We're friends, aren't we?

Vince held still while Clara studied his face. Then she picked up the portrait. "Could we hang this one up?"

Vince nodded. "And there's room for the piano."

Clara closed the sketchbook, slipped the key into her pocket. She whispered, "Can I teach you to play?"

Vince brought Clara's hands to his lips, kissed each fingertip. They sat curled into each others' arms until the bell over the door of Egg Heaven began to chime. Customers filled their regular spots and waited patiently for their eggs.

La Playa

B ell sat on the hard edge of the single bed in the dark, second-floor apartment. She'd pulled the curtains closed against the noon sun, a habit from the house they used to have, all those years of trying to keep Isabella, her mother, comfortable. It hadn't worked. Isabella had suffered anyway. Died of emphysema. The air conditioner was finally turned off, and the quiet cocooned Bell in a gray, dull grief.

The repossession letter arrived a month after the funeral. Bell took the remains of the welfare check and moved into a downtown apartment. Then she found out that at nineteen, she was no longer eligible for welfare.

"You're white. You're young. Get a job," was all the welfare worker said. She pointed Bell to a big chalkboard hanging with index cards. Dock worker. Fish handler. Manual labor. There were other jobs, like receptionist, data entry. But Bell knew she didn't have the right clothes for that. And she didn't know a thing about computers. Her years in high school had been a blur of missed classes, playing hooky to stay home with Isabella because Bell couldn't bear to leave her for one moment.

She spread the want ads over the rough blanket and tapped her finger to the beat of the music coming from beneath her. She lived above a music shop in downtown Long Beach—Licorice Pizza—where she'd tried to get a job when the last of the welfare check wouldn't pay for two more meals. They hadn't hired her because she had no experience. She took a bus to the next place, Bob's Big Boy, where she wasn't asked if she knew what she was doing. The boss handed her a brown apron and told her to work the cash register.

A week later he fired her. The short-change artists had duped her one too many times. He'd yelled, "Are you just too ignorant to spot them? They're all colored!" He was an ugly man with eyes that pointed in different directions. Bell said, "Oh really? What color?" and he fired her on the spot. But that one week gave her enough money to buy scrambled eggs and coffee each morning, and another newspaper.

Every day on her morning walk to get the newspaper, Bell passed the Armed Forces Recruitment Center and its poster, We Want You! One day a tall, thin, black woman in uniform stood leaning in the doorway.

"Hey there, girl. Whatcha up to this hot morning?"

Bell stopped. The woman's lipstick was shiny purple, and her buoyant hair was shaped into a perfect flip. She smiled at Bell. "Hello? Anybody in there?"

Bell blushed and started to move down the sidewalk but the woman said, "You can call me Sergeant Cox. That means I can call you...?"

"I'm Bell."

"So, whatcha doing, going to work or something?"

"I'm looking for a job."

"Well!" Sergeant Cox smiled broadly. "I have just the perfect thing for you. Come on in." She held the door open. "Did you know you have an Uncle who loves you?" She threw back her head and laughed.

Bell stood on the sidewalk, biting her nails.

"Don't be scared. You want work, don't you?"

Bell nodded and followed the sergeant into the office.

Tests had to be taken, background, knowledge, physical status. Bell wrung her hands together while Sergeant Cox explained the procedures for enlisting. She leaned back in her chair and stuck her long legs out, crossing them at the ankle.

"Then there's boot camp, which is a real ride." She stared at Bell, looked her up and down. "How do you feel about tear gas, hmm?" She mentioned South Carolina, sand fleas, debilitating heat.

The Marines sounded like prison. "I just don't know why I should join."

"Education, girl. Don't you want to go to college? A nice girl like you? A nice *white* girl like you?"

Sergeant Cox explained that although the GI Bill no longer provided the cost of a college degree, Bell would be able to put away her pay every month, because, "quite frankly honey, you will be too dog tired to spend it."

Bell already felt dog tired. And an education in what, she wanted to ask. But Sergeant Cox was so beautiful, so clean and tidy, that Bell didn't think her questions would make any sense. She thanked the sergeant and told her she'd think about it.

"Don't take too long, honey," she called after Bell as she went out the door. "It all goes by real fast, you know?"

That night in her room, Bell imagined knots of young women sitting on their cots, laughing together, all smart and tough and strong. Then heads bent at night under lamplight, writing long letters home. She'd be in the bathroom, mopping the floor.

The next morning, Bell resolved to apply to La Playa, a restaurant that ran an ad for "experienced waitress." She knew that waitresses made more than the minimum wage. Bell shrugged off the fact that she had no experience. She could lie. She could cope. She put on her best dress, the one with no holes under the arms, no stains, only a few wrinkles.

Bell stood on the sidewalk in front of the closed wooden door of La Playa. It was a cool day, the sea breeze salty and damp on Bell's legs. Someone had painted a big pink pig on the door. It smiled happily as a wave crashed over its head. She took a deep breath and entered.

The place was empty except for one woman sitting at the counter, bent over her lunch. Air from the ceiling fan lifted a corner of the newspaper spread out next to her plate. The restaurant smelled so good. Bell inhaled deeply, and the woman jumped.

"Oh! You scare me!" she said, sliding off the stool. "Do you want lunch?" She took a menu off the counter.

"I'm here to apply for the waitress job."

"Oh!" The woman laughed a little, and blushed, shaking her head. "I thought you were a customer. Okay. You have experience, *sí?*"

Bell nodded vigorously.

The woman said her name was Linda. She was stocky and black-haired, uneven bangs across her broad pale forehead, eyeteeth a bit too long.

"I own this place with my husband, Pedro. So, you have experience?" Linda gave her a quick once-over. Bell wasn't wearing any nylons, and she hadn't shaved her legs for a few days, because she'd run out of razors. She could feel how loose and shabby her sneakers were. Her face burned.

"What's your name?"

"Bell Kearns."

"*Que lindo*. Your mother gave you a pretty name."

For a moment they just looked at each other. Bell thought Linda might be ten years older than her. Like an older sister. Then Linda went to the counter and patted the stool next to the one she had been sitting on. "Here, sit with me."

Bell climbed onto the stool awkwardly, not quite sure what to do with her hands.

"Do you like *carnitas*?" Linda asked.

"Um, I don't know what that is."

"Pedro!" Linda called out, then said something in Spanish.

A short, squarish, clean-shaven man in wire-rimmed glasses came out of the kitchen smiling. He looked to be about Linda's age. "Nice dress!" he said, setting down a plate in front of Bell.

The aroma of freshly made tortillas, steamy and smelling of corn, rose from a plate heaped with shredded pork, chopped tomatoes and onions, and a tangle of something green.

Bell was starving. She hadn't eaten since the day before, when she'd spent her last few quarters on scrambled eggs at the dingy, cheap restaurant called Breakfast around the block from La Playa.

"What's this?" she asked, holding up a stem of the green stuff.

"Cilantro," Linda said. She and Pedro watched Bell pick at her plate. Then Linda said, "No, *mija*. Like this," and showed Bell how to hold the soft tortilla in her hand, piling the pork and vegetables on top.

"You're pretty skinny," Pedro said. "What's your name?"

"Bell."

"You're experienced, right?"

Bell thought she caught a certain look in his eyes, as if he were asking her something more intimate than her work history. She hesitated. The food tasted so good. Linda seemed so nice.

"*Sí*, she has experience," Linda said. She smiled briefly and placed her hand on Bell's shoulder. "Start today, okay?"

Each morning when Bell arrived, Linda had already been there for hours, cooking two big pots of sauces, one red with chiles, another bright green with tomatillos and onions. Pedro would arrive midday, having brought sacks full of groceries from Los Angeles. Bell asked Linda why Pedro didn't help in the morning when there was so much to do.

"Oh, he is in school," she answered, lifting a huge pot of pinto beans from the sink. "Here, put this on the fire."

"What school? Isn't he too old for school?"

Linda smiled at that. "He is in college, *mija*. Over at the state college, you know, on 7th Street?"

Bell knew where that was. It was the big university in town. Bell wanted to ask more questions, like how Pedro could afford college, and why he wanted to do that, instead of just stay in La Playa and help Linda, who worked so hard. The restaurant was open every single day. But Bell sensed her questions weren't the right ones, that they would only show Linda how stupid she was. College was a topic that never came up at home. Isabella had worked at a furniture factory. Bell's father had left before she ever knew him, so when Isabella got sick, they went on welfare. You can't save up for college on welfare.

But each day Linda helped Bell feel a little less stupid; she taught Bell the correct pronunciations of the dishes they served: dahcos, ahroze con poyo. Every day was a new lesson.

"Green."

"*Verde.*"

"Hot."

"*Caldo.* No, *caliente.*"

"*Bueno!*"

Bell hated to leave at the end of the day. She'd linger, wiping the counter with the white wet cloth one more time, listening to Linda and Pedro murmuring in the kitchen. But inevitably, Linda would call out, "Let's go!" and Bell would switch off the lights in the café, following Pedro and Linda out the back door. She'd stand in the alley as they got into their car and drove away. Then she'd walk back to her apartment, the balmy night breeze carrying diesel exhaust and garbage smells, until she'd reach Licorice Pizza and climb the mildewed carpeted stairs to her room. The day's tips—mostly quarters—always made her feel proud. She often said aloud, "Look, Mom, ten dollars!" Her joy lasted until she turned off the lamp and crawled into the cold bed, her grief pounding like a toothache in every joint.

A month after she was hired, Pedro stood before her and Linda as they ate their after-rush lunches. He rested his hands on his hips, looking officious.

"We have news for you, Bell," Pedro said. Linda was smiling, her long eyeteeth giving her usually calm face a crinkle of glee. "We're giving you a raise."

Bell was speechless. She had never gotten a raise before. All she'd ever gotten was fired.

Pedro said, "Fifty cents an hour. Maybe you can buy some new clothes with the money, huh?"

That night, Bell crawled beneath the scratchy blanket and whispered, "I got a raise, Mom!"

The hot summer turned into an even hotter fall. Even though it had been three months of hard work, Bell still loved entering the café each morning, smelling the coffee and *pan dulce*. With the extra fifty cents an hour, Bell bought dresses from the Goodwill on Pine Avenue. She spent five dollars at Acres of Books on a used copy of Spanish poems with translations on one side of each page, some Spanish-language comic books with their vaguely sexual dangers, and a Spanish-language hymnal.

While Linda read the paper before the morning rush, Bell flipped through the hymnal, imagining singing in Spanish to

Isabella while she slept, hymns like lullabies, the whir and click of the oxygen keeping time.

One day in late October, Linda asked Bell to stay later than usual to do more prep work, because she had to go to Los Angeles to shop. She seemed excited and happy.

"*Día de los Muertos*," she told Bell. "Day of the Dead. We will be closed for three days."

"Did you say day of the dead?"

"*Sí*. It is a fiesta for people who are dead. You will stay late, no?"

While Linda made a fresh pot of coffee, Bell chopped onions.

"*Mija*! Watch out! You are burning your eyes!"

Linda rushed Bell to the sink and splashed cold water on her face. "Wait, are you crying? What is the matter?"

"Nothing. *Nada*." Bell rushed away from Linda and went into the restroom, where she crouched on the floor, trying to stop crying. What would she do for three whole days?

She heard Linda say something to Pedro, and then Linda knocked on the door.

"Back soon, okay? Soak the beans, okay?"

They didn't return until late afternoon. Linda and Bell unpacked the groceries as Pedro leaned against the refrigerator, singing in his clear tenor voice to Linda.

One bag was filled with flowers: orange marigolds and blue coxcomb. Pedro lifted another bag onto the counter and removed rose-colored stalks of sugarcane. Linda held up a little plastic bag to Bell. In it were three toy skeletons made of glow-in-the-dark plastic.

"We bake these into the *pan de muertos*," she said. "Only a lucky person gets the ones with the toy."

Each tiny skeleton was different from the other. Linda lifted the arms of one and made it dance. Linda giggled but then shook her head. "You are so sad, *mija*. I cannot make you laugh today. Well, here. I will teach you something new."

Linda showed Bell all the things she'd be making for the celebration, which she said would last three days and take place on their front lawn. Pedro and some friends had strewn the lawn with black styrofoam gravestones.

"Everything is black, see? I make black *sopes*. Black beans. I love to make the *mole*. It takes a long time." She gestured toward the big clay pot up on the highest counter, a pot they had never used. "I must make it for my grandmother. It is her recipe."

"Does she live with you?"

"No, no, *mija*. She is dead. But she will visit and she must have her *mole!*" Linda laughed, then, her usually blank brow wrinkled with joy. "Go help Pedro, and I will bring you something special."

Bell went out into the café, where Pedro sat whistling at a table by the window. "Can I help?"

Pedro seemed completely absorbed in his work. He shoved a stack of white candles at Bell. "Tie red bows around these," he said.

"Are they for Linda's grandma?"

"*Sí*, of course."

She fingered the red ribbon. There had been candles at Isabella's funeral and the smoke had burned Bell's throat.

After a while, Linda came to the table carrying a serving tray. On it were three white bowls filled with steaming hot chocolate.

"Taste it, *mija*." Linda smiled, and Pedro stopped what he was doing to watch Bell's reaction. The liquid was earthy and rich.

"What do you think?" Pedro asked.

"I love it. Very much."

"Good," Linda said. "Toasted almonds. And cinnamon and vanilla beans. I'll give you the recipe so you can make it for your family."

Bell dampened her face in the steam, the aroma blocking out thoughts of the coming empty days.

While they drank their hot chocolate and assembled pretty artifacts of candle, ribbon, corn and sugarcane, Linda talked about the *Día de los Muertos*, how much she loved the holiday, because she got to make her special dishes. But also because she got to see loved ones long since gone.

"I was an only child. I loved to cook. My family helped me open a small café. That is where I met Pedro. I had a small café in Oaxaca. Pedro was visiting from Puerto Rico."

"It was small all right," Pedro added. "Two tables. Even so, Linda was too shy to wait on them. She always asked someone else to go talk to the people."

"Like who?" Bell wanted to know if she had waitresses before her. She had grown to think of herself as adding something unique to La Playa that Linda needed, something essential and irreplaceable.

Linda laughed, embarrassed. "I would grab any girl playing outside, or walking by the kitchen in the back. 'Hey you!' I would say. 'I will give you pesos if you help!'"

Pedro and Linda laughed. "Then the girl would come in and go up to the people and say, 'What you want?' And then tell me and I just bring them what I make that day. Because, you know, I knew they had come to my little place because they could smell what I was cooking."

"That's how we met." Pedro was grinning at Linda. "I wanted a beer and Linda couldn't find any girls playing around. So I am sitting there, waiting for service, a beer, you know, and out comes Linda with a big plate of tamales. And I thought, hmmm, I must be hungry." Bell could feel him bump Linda's legs under the table. "I was hungry, eh, Linda?" Pedro shot Linda a sleepy-eyed glance, and Linda blushed.

"I loved the little café. I called it La Fuente, because it was right by the fountain in the square. So I call this place La Playa, because it is right by the beach."

Pedro rolled his eyes.

"Well, it is close enough," Linda said. "Bell, you have lived here all your life, here by the ocean?"

Bell told them that yes, she had. "When I was little, my mom and I collected seashells and we painted them with clear nail polish, so that they always looked wet."

"Does your mother still go to the beach with you?"

Bell looked down at her hot chocolate. She shook her head. "Um, not much. Not really."

"We love the beach, too," Linda said. "When Pedro wanted to come to the United States, I said okay but we have to live by the water. He wanted to go to an American school."

"Cal State Long Beach," Pedro said. "Anthropology."

Bell didn't know what anthropology was. It sounded important. Like something Linda and Pedro would be proud of. Bell got a sinking feeling that La Playa would not exist much longer. Why would it, if Pedro was moving on in life, going to the university… probably to become rich and successful. He would take Linda away from the restaurant, give her a better life.

"Linda, don't you think you work too hard?"

"Yes, so I tell my friends when I am gone they must use my recipes so that I will be happy when I visit. Otherwise, I will never come back." She and Pedro laughed.

"But I mean—"

Pedro and Linda stopped what they were doing and looked at Bell, puzzled. "What's wrong, Bell?"

"I mean, this restaurant is really a lot of work. And the customers make you uncomfortable. And, and so maybe you want to do something else with your life."

Linda and Pedro exchanged glances. "Linda loves to cook." Pedro shrugged. "What else should she do?"

"So," Bell continued, nervous, "you won't close La Playa when Pedro finishes college?"

Pedro laughed. "That's a long way away, Bell. More than four years." He laughed again. "What do you think you will be doing in four years, eh? Working here?"

Bell didn't know why he was laughing. Then Linda touched Bell's hair, her shoulder. "Shush, Pedro," she said, patting Bell's arm.

❧

With La Playa closed, Bell decided to have scrambled eggs and white toast at Breakfast. She lingered there as long as she could, but the waitress sat in the back, smoking in the dark, ignoring Bell, so she finally left. It was only seven in the morning, but she didn't want to go back to her empty apartment. She browsed the window of Acres of Books, looking for something new, but there wasn't anything. She had all but memorized the lines of poetry in her book. She read them to Linda every Thursday when they closed, because Pedro was at school then, and he wouldn't laugh at Bell and Linda reading poetry aloud to each other.

The Armed Forces recruiting office was closed, too, but it looked like someone had a light on in the back. Sergeant Cox, probably ironing a blouse.

Bell walked a bit, then ended up in front of La Playa and leaned against the green stucco building, watching the wind blow trash across the asphalt. After a while, she thought she'd better move on, since a police car kept circling the block. Just as Bell was leaving, Pedro's station wagon pulled up to the curb. Linda got out, but she didn't see Bell at first. She was saying something in Spanish to Pedro. Then she came up the walk.

"*Mija!* What are you doing here? This is a holiday! Remember? Is something wrong?" She put her hands on Bell's shoulders and fixed her with her dark steady gaze. "What is it?"

Bell was terribly embarrassed at being caught hanging around, but she was tired and she didn't have anything to do. The days stretched out before her colorless, odorless, deadly silent.

"Tell me, Bell."

"I miss my Mom."

"Where is she?"

Bell pulled away from Linda. Pedro honked and yelled, "Hurry up!"

"Can't I come with you?"

"But where is your mother?"

"Well, she, um." Bell met Linda's gaze. "She died. I tried to keep her alive, but I couldn't do it."

Linda pulled Bell into an embrace. "Oh, *pobrecita.*" It was the first time Linda had done that. Bell pressed her face into Linda's warm neck.

"Why did you not tell me before? When did this happen?"

Pedro honked again, and Linda yelled, "Shush!"

She turned again to Bell, who was trying hard to regain her composure.

Linda shook her head. "You shouldn't keep such secrets. Come with me."

Linda took keys out of her black purse and opened the door to La Playa. She took Bell's hand and led her back to the kitchen. "I forgot something."

They entered the dark kitchen and Bell smelled the familiar sweet smells of flan and chocolate, the acrid aroma of grilled pork, the cushiony steam of boiling *masa*. Linda flipped on the light, and there on the counter on a length of wax paper were dozens of little white skulls sculpted from sugar. Each had a smiling red mouth. They were almost pretty.

"I forgot the most important part!" Linda said, handing Bell a paper sack and piling the little candies into it. Then she said, "Wait here," and Bell stood alone in the brightly lit kitchen, watching Linda run out the front door. A few minutes later, Linda ran back into the café, grinning. "Here," she said, handing Bell a big round golden bun and one of the little skulls.

"It is *Día de los Muertos*, Bell. You must go to your mother's grave and bring her this candy. Did she like candy?"

Bell fingered the sugar skull.

"Then, *mija*, when you need her, she will visit you. Do you understand?" Linda smiled, but Bell could tell she was eager to leave.

"Can't I come with you?"

Linda regarded Bell for a moment. "Look, *mija*," she said. "You work hard. You are a nice girl. You are young." She put the bun and the sugar skull into a paper sack. "I am very sorry your mother is not here today. But do not be unhappy. We have a saying for this holiday: we are not here for a long time, we are here for a good time. Now I have to go. You go, too, okay?"

Bell stood on the street waiting for a bus to take her to Isabella's grave. One pulled up, screeching its brakes, but Bell just stood there until the driver shrugged and pulled the doors shut. She turned and walked down Pine Avenue, toward the beach. Sergeant Cox was pulling up the blinds as she passed.

"Hey, Bell. No work today?"

Bell slowed down but kept walking.

"What's in the bag, girl?"

Bell stopped and opened up the bag. "It's a skull, see?" she said, holding up the candy for Sergeant Cox to inspect.

"Cute. Candy skull."

"It's for *Día de los Muertos*."

"Huh?"

"Day of the Dead. It's…it's a holiday."

Sergeant Cox thought that was pretty funny. She threw back her head and guffawed. "If you think that's a holiday, baby, you'd fit right into the Marines." She shook her head and went back inside the office, muttering, "Day of the dead, indeed."

It wasn't a long walk, just a few blocks to the bluff, then down Ocean to Cherry Park, and then the steep steps to the sand. The park was busy with families having picnics, noisy with Latin rhythms coming from transistor radios. Red, yellow, and green tablecloths covered the many picnic tables, and people were dancing.

The sand was warm at the bottom of the wooden stairs. Bell took off her sneakers and walked down to the water. More Mexican families sprawled across the sand, celebrating. A little girl in a pink bathing suit ran in front of her, giggling and pumping her fists as she ran. Bell watched her fly into her mother's waiting arms. The mother lay back on her towel. She wore a red bathing suit and huge sunglasses, and the little girl sat on her stomach and patted her mother's face. As Bell walked toward the surf, she imagined Linda laughing and carrying trays of her food to family on her lawn, calling out to Pedro to hurry up. "*Ya! Ya!*" Then she imagined sitting on the lawn herself, reciting a poem for the whole family, while Linda smiled at her from the porch.

Bell dragged her toes through the damp hard sand, breathing in time to the long sigh of the outgoing surf, made placid by the lengthy breakwater. She remembered being a child and how the sand rubbed harsh against her thighs, roughing the palm of her mother's hand. And how afraid she was when Isabella would let go of Bell's hand and dash into the water.

After a while, Bell chose a spot on the sun-warmed sand and sat down. She could smell chorizo and roasting corn, and firewood burning in preparation for grilled fish. The October wind was becoming hot. Several young men—black-haired, with glistening brown skin—were playing in the waves, trying to body surf, but mostly laughing and pushing each other underwater.

She closed her eyes and lay back onto the sand. So deep was the strength of the ocean that she could feel it shudder beneath her.

She must have fallen asleep, because one side of her face felt burned from the sun. She sat up. A large group of people with colorful umbrellas stuck into the sand had hung paper flowers along the edges, making it look as though a garden had sprung up in the middle of the beach.

Bell looked out at the ocean and suddenly imagined Isabella sitting up in bed, no oxygen mask on her face, her lips shiny with red lipstick. She was laughing, that laugh Bell remembered from the beach. Her mother would chase the surf out, then turn back toward Bell, toward the beach, trying to outrun the sea. When the wave smashed over her, knocking her sideways into the surf, she'd shout, "Whoopie!"

Bell opened the sack and pulled out the sugary skull. Its mouth was a pretty red. It was beginning to melt from Bell's sweaty palm, and she thought how it would melt with just a little water, or someone's tears. She put the candy in her mouth, sucked on the grainy sugar until it coated her raw throat.

Then she pulled out the bun. It was large, golden and beautiful. She took a big bite and something hard hurt her teeth. A nut shell? A raisin stem? She examined the bun and found a tiny white hand made of bones sticking out of its middle. She pulled at the bones and the bun broke away. A little plastic skeleton lay in her hand, grinning up at Bell, its mouth painted pink.

Bell rose and dusted off the sand from her jeans. A few steps away was a tangle of dank brown seaweed, swirling around an alluvial fan of pebbles. She spotted a foot-long piece of driftwood and picked it up. Sand fleas and tiny black crabs skittered off the wood. Bell carried it back to the paper sack.

She rolled up her pantlegs and picked up the wood and the little plastic skeleton. She walked toward the water, which was leaving streaks of foam as it pulled out to sea. She stepped quickly into the outgoing water, its cold shock making her teeth chatter. She walked further and further out, swaying and almost losing her balance. She held the wood tightly, and when she was waist deep, yards out into the shallow surf, in the calm margin between hot sand and deep ocean, she lay the wood carefully onto the water next to her. She was shivering. Her mouth was filled with the taste of salt sea and mucous and tears. The wood bobbed gently, then inched away, toward the horizon. She lay the plastic skeleton on top of the wood and gave it a little shove.

"*Afortunada*," she whispered, like a prayer.

The wood bobbed down, out of Bell's sight, then back up again, each time further out to sea. The skeleton clung gamely to her throne, a tiny graceful object on the glittering water. Bell watched for a long time, until her shoulders burned and her feet grew numb, but still she could see the speck on the water, heading for the horizon. At last, the tiny skeleton seemed to raise her bony arm and wave. *Hasta luego*. See you soon.

Breakfast

I'm sitting at a small rickety table by the window of this nondescript café, its only sign a half-shattered plastic square that reads BREAKFAST. No name, just what it serves. What I serve. Remarkably, Jesús manages to keep this place open. I don't know why he picked this location, this dingy block of downtown Long Beach, so empty of hope the only life on the sidewalks are the alcoholics ditching into the Algiers Bar across the street. I'm on my break, trying to read a moldy paperback copy of *The Stranger*, drinking coffee I've laced with whiskey from the flask I keep in my apron pocket. The awning of the bar reflects the sun in glaring hot swaths across the asphalt. I lift my cup to drink and in she walks, predictable as the heat of the California sun.

I wonder where she's been today. She looks more alert than usual, though wearing the exact same outfit as she has all month: leopardskin coat, fake-fur collar gray with cigarette ash and dandruff, grimy pink mules. The exposed rough skin of her unshaven ankles makes me sad.

"Hi, Mom," I say.

She ignores me and slowly pushes a stiff lock of yellow-streaked white hair from her broad forehead. She makes no eye contact, although I note a distinct lift of her chin. My mother is too good to be seen talking with the hired help. She glides like a queen toward the counter where Jesús is wiping down the plastic wood-grain paneling. Her hands hang limp. A black patent leather purse dangles off the tips of her long-fingered left hand.

She clears her throat, a rheumy thirty years of tobacco smoke clogging the pipes. Jesús ignores her, and my heart hurts. She's beautiful. How can he ignore her? But Jesús has a business to run, as he explained to me last week, when he dialed 911 to report a vagrant: my mother.

I am worried at how best to proceed because she's earlier than usual and I am not prepared. Yesterday had been a good day, because I had remembered to lay out two quarters on each table before she got here, so that she could come right in, do her work—which is to steal my tips—then get out before Jesús calls the cops. But today everything—the sun, the heat of the whiskey—pushes me to forget just where I am.

I watch her and feel the familiar urge to have a normal conversation, the urge like a gnawing hunger. It must be normal to want that, especially now. I'm getting married this week. It's normal for a girl to turn to her mom at a time like this. It must be. I think: *I'm so glad you came in. I wanted to tell you something. Mike and I are getting married on Wednesday. Do you remember Mike?*

Jesús is now glaring at my mother although he still hasn't spoken to her. He hates it when she comes in. Says it ruins business to have crazies wandering around. I tell him it isn't her fault, she's my mother, what am I supposed to do? We don't argue about it anymore, though. Jesús is only threatening to call the police. He's the last person to want the cops to come in, check things out, study the fake green cards and expired licenses. Besides, he doesn't want me to quit, really, because who else would work in this dull, nameless place?

My mother turns on her heel and heads toward the table in the far right corner. I wince. I have not cleared the table, and the last customers had had a three-year-old who, with both hands, smeared pancake syrup all over everything. I'd noticed the hacking cough of the father, the balled-up napkins containing God knows what.

I want my mother to sit with me, have a cup of coffee, watch the people slip into the darkness of the Algiers Bar.

Remember Mike? We came to see you at the hospital? Mike paid for the taxi fare. He gave you a carton of Lucky Strikes. You told him you were trying to quit so you were going to flush them down the toilet. He thought that was funny. I was relieved, because he'd paid for them out of his tip money, and I thought he'd be mad. And he's so mean when he's mad. But instead he said, "Well, hon, do me a favor and flush them one at a time so they last." You thought that was funny.

Jesús jerks his head over at my mom, then looks pointedly up at the clock. My break is over. I get up and dig through my pockets for some tips. I have about three dollars in change. I approach my mother, who has seated herself at the filthy table.

You're invited. Will you come? Adrian's Wedding Chapel. Adrian said we could invite a witness, but if we couldn't find one, he'd ask his assistant, Hilda. I thought since maybe you were around here, you know, you might stop by. Just a thought. Two o'clock on Wednesday. That's the day after tomorrow.

My mother lights a Lucky Strike and gazes out over the café while I gather the sticky plates and place them on the table next to us. I pull a clean ashtray from my pocket and sit down across from her. Jesús slams something and stomps into the kitchen. I can hear him making a ruckus, something that sounds like forks being thrown into a fan.

Her body smells unwashed. Her black shiny purse sits in front of her. I want to open it up, dig through to the bottom for pennies and Sen-Sen and flecks of tobacco.

"How are you doing, Mom?" I push the quarters in her direction. "I have something to tell you."

She sighs, plumes of white smoke pouring from her nostrils. She looks down at her hands, the backs of her long beautiful fingers tanned from Thorazine and her wanderings beneath the hot sun. Then she frowns. She picks up the quarters. Her brow twists in confusion, her hand resting on the table, palm up, full of quarters. She looks up at me, perplexed.

"Who the hell are you?"

I fold my hands around hers, curling her fingers around the quarters. Her hands are cool and soft.

Will you come? It's me, Laura. Maybe you could play for us. There's an old piano at Adrian's. Nothing much. But all the keys work. I checked. You could play anything you wanted. Chopin. You always loved him.

She is still frowning at me and I can't find any words to speak. I get up and hug her shoulders. Suddenly she pulls me down and we kiss. It is an awkward, quick collision of soft smoky lips. Then my mother turns fierce, her eyes blazing blue and sharp.

She grabs my collar and whispers loudly, "I've got a tip for you. No eye contact." Her eyes fill with tears, the corners of her mouth twist down. She shakes her head slowly. "Just don't look."

I pry her fingers from my collar and my mother's face snaps back to its calm, disdainful beauty. She stands abruptly, drops the quarters into her purse, and marches across the café to the front door. She stands there until Jesús sighs and opens it for her. I run to the window and watch as long as I can the leopardskin back prowling down the street until she disappears around the corner.

It's okay. Never mind. It's no big deal. We don't love each other very much anyway.

Jesús whistles and calls out that it's time for me to get back to work, though there are no customers. The breakfast rush is over. I put my hands into the pockets of my apron, feeling nothing, feeling nothing because I don't know that I will never see her again.

This piano is old.

"Strange that a piano this old and so, umm, untaken care of—sorry, Laura."

"No, that's okay."

"Well..." He crawls out from beneath the legs as if from under a car. His clean blue jeans are worn at the knees, his waist is slender. The piano tuner, Timmy, sits on my carpet, legs crossed Indian-style. He rests his hands and polishing cloth in his lap. His hair is black and curly. His long lashes wave up at me. "It's one of the sweetest pianos I've ever heard." He grins.

I am grateful for this young man, who has come into my home with shiny elegant tools. I always thought it was just my opinion, just my love for this piano, my mother's piano, loving it the way we love the first voice we ever hear, how we come to understand that all other voices are mere echoes of that first sweet voice, a voice I have not heard for fifteen years.

It is a Winter 1937 cottage grand. A cottage grand looks like a regular spinet, but there's something different about its internal workings that I never understood. The chain of events that flows through its intricate systems of levers, springs, and hammers, through felt and wool and wood, makes it different and grand.

We lift the upper lid, swing the tapered arm down to keep it propped open. I gently pull the hinged lid that covers the keyboard all the way out, exposing its insides. Timmy gets to work. He raps a silver tuning fork against his knee, then sticks it between his clenched teeth. He reaches in and secures a tiny wrench, making minuscule adjustments, seeking 440 vibrations per second.

I ask Timmy what happens to a piano as it ages. He explains that first the leather and felt compact so that the action becomes uneven and less responsive. Rattles and squeaks develop.

"All the action parts become worn out," he says, tapping middle C. He frowns. "Hmmm. The keys are getting wobbly." I want to stop his hand from tapping the key, from using up its strength.

"It gets worse," he continues. "Hard to believe, but the strings may actually break." He plucks a rusty B-flat string and its dull thud silences us for a moment.

"Some pianos just die." Timmy leans toward the hammers and sighs. "The big failure is hidden—look, just below the surface of the cap." He points to the cap, fingers it, and in the rising dust I smell decades of cigarette smoke and my mother's breath.

When he's finished tuning, we examine the ornate cabinet. Its color shifts from one side to the other. The side closest to the fireplace is paler than the rest. He rubs his finger into a round cigarette scar, around the water-stains of the alcoholic years I spent trying to rid myself of Mike.

To distract Timmy from the damage I tell him, "I clean the keys with curdled milk."

He shoots me a glance. "Oh, I think I heard about that. Something about lactic acid?"

He encourages me to reconsider restoration. "I know it's expensive, but it's such a lovely instrument. Still. She's worth it."

When the piano tuner leaves, I pull out the bench. I've draped it with a homely pink rug to cover up how it is cobbled together with too many thin nails since that day ten years ago—when Mike broke it into pieces against the wall, then came after me—when one post-blackout morning the damage he did to the piano, to me, finally entered my consciousness and I made calls. The police came. I met Margaret, a therapist, in a hospital rehab hallway.

I rub the dampness of last night's bottle of whiskey off the coffee table. I only had one, well just the one bottle. Just a small one when I got the letter; when I heard the news, then called Margaret: *What should I do?*

Thirty or more books of music line the shelf above the piano. I choose Chopin's raindrop prelude. The prelude is not a piece I'm familiar with, so I proceed slowly, *addolorato*. But even in this dirge I can hear the water, the life force. The piano tuner told me this piano is now only in tune with itself, accurate pitch no longer possible for its aging body.

My mother had schizophrenia and perfect pitch. She'd call out "G" when the phone rang, "F" at the doorbell. As I clumsily, slowly, begin the prelude's *arpeggio* down the keyboard, like so many drops of rain on a lonely night, I try to remember if this piano—her piano—was always weak in its pitch, and if so, was this what drove her mad, knowing the way she did what constituted a perfect sound? I do not know what drove her from me that last day near the Algiers Bar. I do not know what killed her. Tomorrow, because Margaret says I must, I shall find out.

When I enter the medical records office of Metropolitan State Hospital, a man rises from a desk. The nameplate on the desk reads Miguel Torres. He is the records clerk who answered the phone when I called weeks before, when Margaret and I decided it was time to know. He waves his hand at a long table. On it is a stack of folders twelve inches high. I stand in the middle of the room, rubbing the backs of my hands. They burn when I am afraid. The smell of dust and mold is familiar and sad.

A woman wearing a white muumuu with pink hibiscus comes into the room. I think she is a patient. She says hello. She stands close to me and then I think she isn't a patient, because she smells fresh and wears socks and white tennis shoes with her laces tied. She smiles at me and motions to the tower of my mother's records.

"Go ahead, honey. Tell us which ones you want. We'll copy them for you."

Miguel comes back in and hands me a box of paper clips. "Sixteen admissions, miss," he says. "What do you want?"

Everything, I want to tell him. How can he ask me that? Why can't I just pick up this stack and walk back to my car and drive away? Miguel leaves the room again, and the woman touches my shoulder. "Five cents a sheet." She shakes her head and sits down at a typewriter table and begins to poke fingers at the keys.

I open the first manila folder. There is a small black-and-white Polaroid of my mother's face, an intake photo of a woman in the throes of a nervous breakdown. Her hair hangs longer than I remember it. Her eyes seem sleepy and she is almost smiling, as if she has just had good sex or heard the voice of God.

I did not expect to find my mother, not like this; I have been without her for so long I assumed all traces of her life had disintegrated into dust. I had thought, wrongly, that this hospital had closed, that the tools that shocked my mother, burned her memory down to ash, the so-called machinery of cure, had been bulldozed.

When I received the notice from the hospital that her records were to be purged (how did they find me?), I called Margaret, whom I had only seen a few times, back when I was disintegrating into alcoholism, before these blank years of sheer coping. Margaret asked, how did she die? I told her I did not know, that she had disappeared one hot day while I was at work.

But here is my mother, stapled to a form. I quietly yank the photo from the page and slip her into my purse. For an hour I turn the pages slowly, finding more photos, delaying the inevitable final pages. Miguel comes back into the room and taps his watch.

"We have to get started copying or we won't be able to give you anything," he threatens. I relinquish my stack to him and he carries it back into the bowels of the archives.

When I arise to leave, my hands not full enough of what I came for, of what I crave, the woman in the muumuu says, "Wait, honey. I've got something for you." She opens a drawer and hands me a piece of paper. It's a recipe for Harvey Wallbangers.

"It's different now," she says. "It's not shameful anymore."

I'm not sure what she's referring to. I thank her for the recipe and touch her shoulder lightly as she turns back to the typewriter. She bats my fingers away and bends toward her work. I notice, then, the key dangling from her wrist. She's not a patient. At least, not anymore.

On my way home I stop only once, for bourbon. The red blinking light of a message greets me as I unlock the door to my house. It's Margaret, asking me to call her. I do.

"Did you get the records, Laura?"

"Yes." I move to the refrigerator and try not to make any noise as I drop ice cubes into a glass. My hand is shaking. "Not all, though."

"Call me if you want to later, will you?"

I hang up, and my hand stays on the phone for a long time. Chopin is playing in my head and I am riveted to the spot, one hand around a glass of booze, one on the phone. It is my mother's crazed rendition of the minute waltz, which she played in thirty seconds flat, and I see before me the frenetic dance I would dance behind her as she sat at our piano, the sweet oceanic dread of the waltz making me weep with her.

When the music fades I bring the hospital records to the couch. I hold tight to the glass. Finally, I begin to turn the pages.

There she is again, more photos. They are askew, as if she could not stop moving. In one she looks like a mean parrot; in another her hands blur as she makes the sign of the cross across her polka dot blouse. The blouse is on backwards. In another her eyebrows are lifted into a dramatic *V* as if to plead, "What am I doing here?"

I begin to disbelieve. It is all so unreliable. I remember my mother as young and beautiful, not sick and dying. I thought she was not mad, just *agitato* and *rhapsodic*. As I read through these records, I see that even the orderlies have written down the wrong year in places; that the nurse mistook her sleeping form for another patient; that a doctor noticed she had *some* musical ability.

Then I am stopped by one last photo. It is the leopardskin coat. It is the stiff white hair.

The phone rings and it's Margaret again.

"Are you all right?"

"Yes."

"Do you want to talk?"

I shake my head, but she can't hear that. I want to tell her I am grateful she called but that I have to go now, the news has arrived and my mother is dying. I must attend to her funeral. I hang up, hoping she understands.

I turn to the final page. The handwriting is elegant for a doctor. I wonder briefly if he was an artist, then I read that it was lung cancer that killed her. She drowned in ash.

The physician wrote, "All I could do for this patient was give her a cigarette, for which she was obviously grateful."

Yes, she would have been. What a kind gesture.

The phone rings. I push the glass away. The ice makes a tinkling sound, and the smell hovers, like smoke.

Delgado's Family Mexican Restaurant

Love the sand in my toes, how 'bout you?" I glanced over at Jacinto, who was already taking off his shoes. We had just gotten back from a trip to the beach, to Jacinto's Aunt Bell's restaurant, La Playa. My relief at being back home in the desert was tainted by the ongoing argument. I straightened out the blankets in the back of the pickup while Jacinto stretched his legs.

We sat in our favorite spot on the desert floor, between two of my beloved Joshua trees, each with prickly limbs pointing in five different directions at once. I studied Jacinto's reaction to my suggestion, knew he was thinking hard about it. I ached with longing at Jacinto's graceful form perched on the boulder, the severe blue of California sky a backdrop to his black hair. I prayed to the trees to make Jacinto agree: no test. Never.

While Jacinto cogitated, poked at the sand with his finger, a little gust of a hot spring breeze lifted a feather of his hair. I knew Jacinto was trying to envision the future, his sloe-eyed vision of the possibilities, but more importantly, the pitfalls, the dragons, the strangers with guns and arrows. If he had one at hand, I knew, Jacinto would at this moment be gazing into a large crystal ball, his bottom lip atremble, the Fates and Furies circling madly about his head.

I pressed my palms to Jacinto's cheeks, caught his dark, steady, worried gaze. I could feel his muscles tense, his jaw tighten.

"It's simple enough, Hyacinth. Do the math. Suss the proof. Line up the eggs in the basket."

Jacinto nodded, rested his forehead against my chest. "Say it again, Sam?"

I knelt on the ground and took Jacinto's bare feet into my hands. "It won't make any difference. At least, the kind of difference you think it might. Which is the whole point."

"But—"

"Because it's all the same thing, Jack." I kneaded his instep, brought his feet onto my lap, pushed down. "A mere process of elimination. You've got two cowboys, right? One's got the blue hat, one's got the pink hat. Just kidding. The other one's red."

Jacinto smiled. "Lavender."

"You traffic in the shopworn, my dear. Anyway, two guys, two hats, one blue, one lavender. That's door number one. Then you've got two guys, two hats, but they're both blue. That's door number two. Then you've got two guys, two lavender hats. Door number three. See?"

Jacinto shook his head. "I have no idea what you're talking about."

I sighed heavily, for dramatic effect. "It doesn't matter what color the hats are. It doesn't matter who's wearing what. You've still just got two guys with two hats."

"Just? I'm crushed. And I still don't know what you mean. I *am* one of the guys, right?"

"Of course. That's what I tell all my friends. I say, hey, see my lover over there? Hyacinth? He's just one of the guys."

Jacinto reached out his hand to me and I pulled him up into my arms, nuzzled.

He whispered, "Let's just get it over with, Sam. Quit chewing on it. Let's just get it done. Now, can we have *safe* sex? As in now?"

"Can we? Ah, such irony. Such pithy repartee." I kissed Jacinto's neck. "We may," I murmured. "We might. We ought to."

"Jesus fucking Christ, do you ever stop talking?"

I dragged Jacinto into the truck bed, onto the sleeping bag and crawled on top of him, covering him with my burly shoulders, my oversized hands and thick legs.

"Only when there are better things to do."

I walked toward the corner of the boulevard that led past the strip, past Delgado's Family Mexican Restaurant, home of my newly adopted career: waiting tables. Good enough for Jacinto and his family, good enough for Sam. I loved swaggering up to the table full of ladies in polyester, winking and nudging them toward the fish tacos, "crunchy in all the right places."

The afternoon was cooling, only 78 the digital bank sign blinked as I waited for the light to change. I leaned against a lamppost, trying to look sexy but missing by a smidgeon. Too many hours at Delgado's today, too many for this forty-five-year-old rapidly aging self.

I gazed down the boulevard, thought again about the miles barren of vista and feeling. Or so I had thought when the doc recommended getting away, far away. Palpitations, breathlessness, *your heart is getting weak* the doc said, and I drove my SUV away from Utah, away from the marriage and my regular guy life, to this arid town.

The street was filled as usual with passersby, tall and busty drag queens, hoards of touring families, an entire genteel class of closeted gay men and wealthy Republicans, although I still could not sort them out, thought perhaps they all—queens, families, left and right—had come, like me, to this scorching desert having followed some mythical signage in the queer shapes of prickly trees. Such a strange place, so quiet, so quiet, once out in the desert. I loved the dry windswept cholla-choked hills, the heat, the sun. And I loved Jacinto, was in love for the first time in my life.

I crossed the street and entered the blinding darkness of Tony's Pasta and Steak, sliding into my regular booth near the bar. I nodded toward Lou, the bartender, who poured bourbon neat and brought it over to me.

"Louie Louie, oh baby." I feigned a punch to Lou's shoulder.

"Knock it off. Christ." Lou lumbered back to his bar.

Jacinto was taking an order from five overly tanned men, all swilling scotch. I admired Jacinto from behind, how the white apron strings crossed his narrow waist and dangled down his beloved backside, how his shoulders seemed like a single two-by-four, so straight across were they. That pain came, then, in the middle of my chest. I knew exactly what it was. Just a muscle sore from its workout. *Ain't no cure*, I hummed, *ain't no cure*, as Jacinto worked his shift.

"My friend, Samuel," Jacinto was telling the men, who were wringing him for insider tourist info, "we go together to the Sunday market." He was plying his version of a Mexican accent, though he was *so* So Cal. I loved the show, knew Jacinto was putting it on just for me.

"Samuel, my friend? He loves the Joshua trees."

The men knocked back their scotches, asked about golf.

"Oh, if you stay long, you will see many women golfers, all good friends of Dinah Shore."

The men liked this, thought they would get lucky. I hoped they would leave Jacinto a drunken pile of ten-dollar bills.

While Jacinto strode back and forth across the dark, garlicky restaurant, I flipped through the brochure I had brought. The Ramona Pageant was coming soon, first week of April. It would be one year from the day we met, and I wanted to return to the scene of the luscious crime. It would be our anniversary present. Take our minds off things for a day.

Latex, latex. How crazy to end up like this, the paradise of heat locked inside a boundary, the worthless boundary. No boundary in the history of the world ever stopped anything. In fact, my awkward fumbling with the condom seemed to fuel Jacinto's desire, and he had more than once—to my childlike gratitude—ripped the thing from my fist.

Lou set another double in front of me, and the alcohol filled me with an unbearable sense of well-being. Fuck the fucking test, who cared? But Jacinto had insisted, bawled like a hungry baby, said it was not an option if we were to continue on, had to get tested, had to know.

I downed the bourbon, burning my throat. I had meant to keep it to myself, what finally, stupidly, occurred to me, occurred to me right in the middle of the fight: that only one test was needed.

And what it would test was not reducible to a mere human virus. No, it would test the tensile strength of our bond, this past-midlife empyrean I had lifted into the moment I had spotted Jacinto at the soft-drink stand at the outdoor melodrama of Ramona. I wandered aimlessly while Spanish dancers twirled their skirts and the pageant took a break, the tragic Ramona and more tragic Alessandro reapplying makeup in their tents, and there he was, a sinewy square-shouldered black-haired god, sunglassed and sipping a date shake. A little boy in a sombrero sat next to Jacinto. I took the place next to the boy.

All my life I had only considered this option in fevered, half-remembered dreams, and yet, while all else fell apart behind me—my marriage, my construction company failing in Utah—I knew, instantly, that Jacinto was the one. Small talk with the little boy, one of five of Jacinto's nephews, about family, about Jacinto being out his whole adult life, and soon it was only the two of us, heat like flame licking between us. I had believed when I was a child that Joshua trees pointed the way to heaven. Now as I lived among them, walked among them on Saturdays, holding hands with Jacinto like stupid teenagers, I touched their spines to see if I would bleed, if I were still walking on this earth.

I shook the ice cubes in my glass, savored the cold in my mouth. The argument had been a bad one, probably the worst one. It was Jacinto's fear that started it. I could hardly stand the patent unfairness of my gentle and steady lover falling beneath the weight of such dire predictions, such bad math. I had raged on and on until Jacinto all but slugged me. I finally said it. "Only one test, Jack, me or you. Do you understand?" *Did he understand?*

Jacinto waved over to me, his shift over, just some sidework to be done.

"Let me see." Jacinto slipped into the booth next to me. "Oh, Ramona. I didn't realize it was so soon." He put his arm around my shoulders and squeezed hard, then read the brochure. "'America's oldest outdoor drama.' Our anniversary, Sammy. Thank you."

We had decided at last it would be me, for no other reason than to end the fighting. So three times that week I walked up to the door of the family planning clinic, and three times turned and walked away, because each time I could not shake the illogic of getting tested at all. If I were to test positive, it would be an almost certainty that so would Jacinto. Latex would then magically disappear from our lives. *Adiós.* But if I were to test negative, well, I had nothing left to protect, so what did it matter? My heart was already colonized; nothing could part me from Jacinto's side. The immensity of the safety issue was nonsense. Love was the most dangerous equation in the universe and I was so awash in the incendiary heat of love I could actually feel, every night, the earth swoon away from the sun.

Tuesday, enchilada night at Delgado's. While I waited for José to put up my orders, I surveyed the boulevard from the plate-glass window. The clinic was across the street.

"Order up," José called out, and when I turned to pick up the platters of food, I spotted Jacinto coming out of the clinic.

My palms broke into a sweat. *Just stay cool. One platter at a time, one thing on your plate at one time.* As Jacinto came across the street, I set the food in front of a party of three women. The door opened. The bells tinkled as Jacinto entered.

I swallowed hard. "Busy day, I see."

Jacinto fixed his gaze on me and for a moment, neither of us spoke. I heard the sound of the fryer, the click of fork to plate, smelled the cilantro, felt the floor beneath me, but nothing, nothing was more blood-filled and real than Jacinto's presence before me.

Jacinto nodded slowly. Then one of the women said, "Excuse me?" and I tore myself away from my lover's hypnosis.

Jacinto sat at the table along the wall, read the newspaper while I worked my shift. By the time I turned the sign on the door to CERRADO, my pounding heartbeat had finally subsided and I felt I could reasonably sit across from my lover, who had actually entered the clinic across the street and put us both in harm's way.

But when I finally sat across from Jacinto, this beautiful man who had now pulled us both too near the flame, I felt sick with rage. Before I could speak, before I could say, *Do you not understand the concept of risk?* Jacinto said, "Bad news, Sam."

And suddenly I felt nothing, my heart still as death. I did not even feel hate. I folded a napkin, pressing my fingertips into the folds. "Not possible. Global warming? That's as bad as news can get."

Jacinto grabbed my hands. "Listen to me, please? You were right. All along."

"You seem to be saying something significant, Jack, but just exactly what it is eludes me."

He sighed deeply, ran his fingers through his glossy hair. "Look." He turned the newspaper toward me. "The Joshua trees are dying. It's the drought. The friggin' endless drought."

The newspaper lay on the table before me, and I would have read the news if my eyes weren't filling with tears.

Jacinto pulled the newspaper back, pushed it aside. "They're being eaten from inside out. By thirsty rabbits."

"Don't make me laugh."

Jacinto grabbed my hands again. I felt my heart contract, but resisted the urge to press it. "Thirsty rabbits? That's pretty funny, Jacinto. I must be rubbing off on you."

Jacinto smiled. "From day one."

"Ah, Alessandro."

"No, Sam. I'm Ramona. You never get that straight."

"I never do."

"Thank God."

"I do, dear. Every single blessed day."

That night, I couldn't shake the newspaper image of the trees—their bark flayed, the colonizing animals sucking the life from their limbs, the way the trees seemed to be toppling in slow motion, like me, like the crazy shift of sand beneath the boulevard, shifting, swallowing lives whole. I lay in the dark trying to steady my breathing. That pain, that familiar jolt to my heart, ever present.

"Sam, listen. Wake up." Jacinto was sitting up. "We should talk."

"No."

"Please just let me speak, Sam."

I rolled onto my back, knowing I could not stop myself from touching Jacinto's face, the swell of his mouth, the warm rise of his chest. "I'm sorry. It's—"

"Quiet, Sam, okay?"

I wanted to shut my ears to what Jacinto would say, because I knew it would be less than he meant it to be, knew that there was always too much life between the skin and the cells, between the bark and the moisture, to be uttered to the one person who needed to hear it most. Jacinto was speaking but I couldn't make out the words. All I could think about was how lost we had gotten. Where were the trees? Where?

I pulled Jacinto down around me. "The trees," I sobbed, "the trees."

"But Sam, one hundred years. Only one hundred years and they'll be back. Can you last that long? Will you last that long for me? *Por favor,* my favorite cowboy? I will for you, I swear to God, Sam."

In the dark, I felt Jacinto curl his body around me, slender leg beneath my heavy thigh, fingers pushing under my back, head heavy on my chest, until I could see nothing, hear nothing except the pounding of my own heart, its stunning particularity holding out hope, one beat at a time.

MarDel's Diner

It was the end of summer and the porch trellis was shaggy with wisteria. Unusual, Alex thought, as he reached the porch steps. Why hadn't she pulled the flowers from the vines yet, stuffed them into glass vases? Was she already too weak? He yanked off a withered blossom, tossed it behind the bougainvillea, which was fluttering as usual with salmon-colored petals.

He checked his watch, stepped up to the door and knocked. He wiped the back of his neck with a handkerchief and waited. No response. He knocked again. Nothing. He pressed his ear to the door, certain a murmur—her voice—came from inside.

"Laura?" he called, but she didn't answer, although he thought he detected a slight pause in the murmur. He checked his watch again. Exactly 11:30 a.m. Exactly when he said he'd arrive. Why wasn't she answering the door?

Exasperated, mostly because of the heat, he told himself, not because Laura may have completely forgotten he was coming— and when that thought crossed his mind, Alex felt a lump rise in his throat. Was he still so unimportant to her? Then why had she called him, called Alex, not someone else? Surely there was a space in her heart carved precisely to fit her husband?

The trip had seemed longer than usual, the highway busier than it should have been, the day hotter than he had planned. It was 103 degrees when he left the Inland Empire and headed west, toward the beach and Laura, who was dying, and not just dying of the heat.

She could have forgotten him entirely, given the circumstance.

I'll be there, whatever you need, Laura, he had said into the message machine two days before. She had called and he had picked up the phone and her voice—husky as it always was in the early morning—had stunned him awake. She hadn't called him in all that time, not since the final call three years before.

He had been embarrassed at the scratchiness in his voice. He was alone in bed, as always. Maybe he had been dreaming about a woman's body when the phone rang, or maybe it was just Laura's voice, the cadence, the timbre, as if she were whispering in his ear. For a moment Alex thought he was still asleep, having one of those luscious visceral dreams that stick like real memory. Then he felt the vacant, cold space beside him. He sat up. There couldn't be a good reason for the call. His stomach sank. "What's wrong?"

She hesitated for so long his heart stumbled in arrhythmia. He rubbed his chest, thought about how he could get away from work, how long she might need him. It never even occurred to him to say no.

"Breast cancer. I'm just, I just—"

"Are you sure?"

"Yes." She sighed deeply.

Alex closed his eyes, pressed the receiver hard against his ear, pulled the warm blankets over his head and pretended she was right there on the bed next to him. "The thing is, I find out next week what the treatment will be."

Alex felt inordinately angry and knew he was about to say the wrong thing.

"You must tell me everything, Laura. Right now."

"I don't know. Oh, I just shouldn't have called you." She hung up.

After a few moments, after he was able to push away from a spiraling nausea, he called back. She didn't pick up and he listened to the ringing, picturing her in her silk slip, covering her ears, angry and scared. He hung up, then called back. This time the message machine went on. He said he was coming and when.

And here he was on her doorstep.

Alex knocked again. Again he thought the muted voice paused, and he felt a flash of anger. "Laura?" he called out. "I'm here." Silence.

He stood on the porch looking out at the old neighborhood. She'd kept the house, changed it some. The paint was lighter, Navajo white, the trim Navajo red. He fingered the peeling paint with a little hopeful rush that Laura had no man around to take care of things. The murmur behind the door began again, and he felt foolish just standing there.

It had been at least three years since he had seen her, and while he supposed it was always awkward and unpredictable when ex-spouses decided to meet again, especially at one of their homes, especially when one has just received word that the other was going to die … still, he had promised. He kept his promises, not that she ever believed that. He had driven hundreds of miles, taken a leave of absence from work, just in case.

He walked slowly to the sidewalk, expecting Laura to open the door and call out to him. At the sidewalk he stopped. The heat shimmered off the asphalt of the street, just as it had that last morning. He felt as helpless now as he had then, impotent against Laura's stony resolve to excise him from her life. And now, her death.

If she wouldn't come to the door, then perhaps he could call her. He scanned the street and thought how pretty it was still, every trim lawn edged with impatiens and sky-blue lobelia, yellow portulacas and cactus. Laura had insisted on this small neighborhood too many blocks from the beach because the sound of the surf kept her up at night. At first Alex was skeptical, but the regularity of the street—same postman, same dogs, same paperboy—quickly cemented his own self-image: Alex, a married man.

He thought perhaps that tiny café, MarDel's Diner, might still be in business. If so, they'd have a phone.

There was no point in driving, since there was probably no place to park. The neighborhood so oddly zoned—a row of stucco houses, a mom-and-pop store with an apartment on top, a gas station, narrow streets, mostly one-way. He walked down Roswell past the elementary school and rounded the corner on 4th Street.

Alex entered the tiny stucco café and there was Dell, the cook. Dell looked exactly the same, like a barrel in overalls. Then, as if Alex had never left, as if it were a Sunday years before and he and Laura had made their sleepy way to the café, Dell called out, "The usual?"

Mary, Dell's wife, came sashaying into the café from the back door, her enormous girth covered in a flowery shift. Mary always made Laura smile because Mary was clearly a sunny, happy person, even though she and Dell spent every day in this tiny space superheated by the fiery grill, serving scorched bacon and fried eggs to a handful of people in the know. Laura had shown Alex this place under protest: too divey, he had thought, even for a lazy summer Sunday. She pressed him and he became addicted quickly to the warm, smoky smells, the dance Dell and Mary did, spatulas waving, Mary ducking under Dell to grab coffee mugs and Tabasco, Dell flipping eggs onto plates.

Mary grinned at Alex, her cheeks pushing her black eyeglasses up against her eyes. Alex wanted to cry. He had loved these mornings. He had loved his wife, their routine. It had all been enough for him. Which Laura never believed, even before it became less than true.

"Mary," he called out over the noise of the exhaust fan. "Do you have a phone I could use?"

She smiled and waved a hand toward the back door. As Alex moved toward the door, Dell yelled, "No, sit and eat!"

"I can't," Alex said. "I'm sorry."

The alley was hotter than hell, the black asphalt sticky. Alex was drenched in sweat. He lifted the receiver, dropped in the coins, and punched in Laura's number. The phone rang and rang. He dialed again, and again it rang, he counted twenty times. He hung up, looked at his watch. 12:15. He went back inside and headed toward the front door, past Mary and Dell, who stared at him, both standing with their hands on their hips, huge twins.

"Excuse me," he said, "I have to go. I—" Alex swallowed hard. "I'm here to meet an old friend, but we're missing each other, so..." He rushed out.

He walked quickly past the laundromat, empty from the heat, past the liquor store, again past the elementary school. When he got to Laura's house—their old house—he paused, overcome with nervousness, dizzy from the heat. This wasn't turning out how he'd planned, although he truly had only planned on hugging his wife again, maybe more. On the freeway his fantasies had wandered too far. He had loved Laura as simply as anyone could, that was all. After spending his twenties and thirties in an endless series of dramatic, lustful, intense couplings, Alex found Laura working at a bookstore, her own store, and effortlessly left his old life, like a seal leaving the hot dry sun, slipping into a deep, cool, watery world.

Laura, it turned out, was plagued by mistrust, mostly because of other men who had met Laura long before they could understand how lucky they were. Alex understood them, which made Laura nervous. *Why do you condone them,* she would cry, *how they treated me?* Alex had a hard time explaining himself, that he hated that anyone had ever hurt her, but that she should understand they were boys, they were busy making every single action of their day, every encounter, a proving ground. He himself had been the same, before Laura came into his life. But Laura would shake her head at this, walk stiffly from the room. Alex would call after her, *Laura, look at me, I am a man with the capacity to say yes, forever, to another human being.*

He stood on the sidewalk and said aloud, calmly, "Laura. I'm here." He walked up the steps and knocked on the door. He stood back, sure Laura would finally realize how late it was, that it was probably Alex knocking, and unlatch the screen. He closed his eyes and slowly counted to five. Then to ten.

He hated doing it, but he tried the knob and there it was again. Her voice.

"Laura?" Alex pulled on the locked door, rattled it, slammed his palm against it. "Laura!"

Silence. He inhaled deeply to calm himself, and sat down on the porch steps in the cooling shadow of the limp wisteria. He felt watched, hoped he was. Hoped Laura was peering out at him, her ex-husband, sitting patiently on her front steps, waiting.

And waiting for what, he began to wonder. For the sound of the lock turning, the creak of the door, the relief of the darkness inside their home, Laura, wrapping her strong slender arms around his neck, pressing into him? His eyes watered with the thought. Would she be frail? Was the air conditioner working still? The one he had replaced and then repaired and then repaired again against the Southern California heat? He would ask her that. About the air conditioner and the wisteria, once she opened the door.

He tried to think rationally. Was she too weak to come to the door? Had she forgotten, if not him exactly, then the day or the time? Or worse—but no, he wouldn't even entertain for a moment the thought that she might be deliberately trying to hurt him. Not now, not after so long. She had called him, after all, given him one more chance with her thin voice and her terrible news. One more chance in the muddle of lonely dull days since she had told him she would never recover, from him.

Alex didn't want to cry, not out in public on this, his old porch. Action was needed. He decided to walk back to MarDel's and try to call her again, keep calling until she finally picked up the phone.

When Alex walked in, Mary and Dell stopped what they were doing.

"I'm sorry," he said. "I'm trying to see Laura."

"Oh," Mary said. "Laura never comes in here anymore. Right, Dell? We never liked her anyway."

Dell laughed. "She's joking. We love her. She was here yesterday."

Alex wanted to ask if she had been alone, but didn't. He also wanted to ask how she looked. Was she tired? Had she eaten?

Mary read his mind. She planted both palms on the counter and shook her head, looking Alex dead in the eye.

"Skinny broad, that one. Yuk."

Dell shouted over his shoulder, "She only ate one pancake. One bacon. I charged her one dollar."

Alex's head hurt, from Mary's cigarette smoke, the noise of the exhaust fan, the heat. Maybe he needed to eat. Maybe she had turned off the phone, the ringing hurting her somehow. Or maybe she was counting, too.

"May I please have a couple of eggs?"

"Oh sure, you gonna eat now?" Mary twinkled at him, slapped a napkin and fork before him. Poured lemonade from a pitcher and filled the glass with ice. "Dell! Get this guy a sandwich!"

Alex had forgotten that part—how Dell and Mary sometimes just gave you what they thought you needed. It was the strangest behavior he had ever witnessed in a diner, even one as tiny and obscure as MarDel's. Laura's love for the place was iron-like. Unmoving, unbendable. Alex often thought it was the mere presence of the sweating couple, so clearly at home with each other, like sister and brother.

Her love for him, however tender and on fire the first year, seemed to melt before his eyes, transforming into constant accusations and later, when the accusation was finally true, a brief, sullen silence ending with Alex heading east to a new life. As Alex chewed on his BLT, mayonnaise dripping onto the plate, he remembered how long he had tried to convince her that he was absolutely clear, clear in a Zen-like, pure way, about his commitment to her.

Alex watched Dell and Mary shuffle around the counter. Dell hummed, and Mary made little clucking sounds. Alex could feel their familiarity, he could smell it. He watched them and knew that Dell probably slept on his back and snored, while Mary rested her matted hair against his soft huge chest. Laura's head always startled Alex with its weight against his arm, its warmth, the pillow smell of her tangled hair in the morning.

It had been only once. One brief night after work. Once in three years and with a perfect stranger, a woman alone in a bar, not someone Alex knew or cared about. Just a warm body to cry into after Laura had once more wept with rage that Alex was cheating on her, pleaded with him to leave her, to just get it over with. The noise, the heat, it all pressed too hard and he ran to the car, drove to the air-conditioned Seaspray Tavern. The darkness and the coolness and the leaden weight of bourbon slowly dimmed it all. When he woke up, it was morning and he was alone. He drove home, knowing what lay in store: an empty, echoing canyon where his world had been.

Alex stopped chewing. That was it. That's what this was about. She would make it impossible for him to keep his promise: till death us do part. Laura would not allow Alex the chance to become her faithful lover. She would rob him of that final intimacy. Tears welled up in his eyes. For Laura. For himself. He pictured her under a white sheet in a cold room bright with chrome and humming with machines, alone, twisting in pain, hugging her thin arms around her bandaged chest. He thought about Laura's skin, her sex, how she often cried when she came and how scary that was at first, until he just let it go. Until he realized that the only thing he could do about her anguish was to lie still with her until she became so exhausted she fell asleep in his arms.

Alex set his sandwich down and slowly wiped his face. Mary lifted his plate away. She peered into Alex's face.

Alex gripped Mary's hand. She frowned. "Are you drunk?" she said. "What's the matter with you?"

Dell waddled over. "Hey! Leave my wife alone!" Then Dell laughed, but Mary shoved her elbow into his side. "Shut up, stupid." Dell shrugged and went back to the stove.

Alex let go of Mary's hand and pulled his wallet out to pay. "Forgive me. I'm sorry."

"Don't pay." She slapped his hand away from his wallet. "Where have you been? It's all different without you." Mary smiled sweetly. Dell stood behind her looking concerned. "You were our favorite couple."

Alex put his wallet back into his pocket and nodded, not able to speak. He slowly pushed himself outside, back out into the hot day.

As he walked back to the house, a breeze had finally come up, and he walked slowly, letting the wind cool the burning in his eyes, his throat. Two bluejays overhead squawked at each other, such a familiar sound.

He climbed the porch steps and plucked at the faded wisteria blossoms.

It had been his job to feed the birds, fill the tubes with sunflower seeds all year long. Every morning before work. And while he poured the seeds into the feeders, the jays would stand together on the fence, yelling at him to hurry up. Some mornings, especially in the first year, he'd stand on the porch and count: one—Laura, two—the birds, three—this place on earth. He knew he didn't deserve the happiness. Three years later, he tossed it into the blue California sky.

He listened to the silence inside, saw suddenly that the ceiling fan was on because the curtains were lifting, barely, but lifting rhythmically. She had always turned it on when Alex came home for lunch. *How is your day going,* she would ask. And, even in the last days, he hated going back out the door, into the world, away from her.

He sat down on the porch. The concrete was cool and familiar. The sea breeze swirled in silent, soft gusts, like the faint gush of blood through his heart, pulsing, pulsing with hope.

An hour later, behind him, the screen door creaked open.

Northwoods Tavern

Never underestimate the kindness of feminist lesbians. A month after Hannah left me, they sent me a brochure. "You're invited to the Women's Music Festival." How uncanny that they would invite me right at that moment, right when shame at being dumped by Hannah drenched each of my mornings. The annual woman-only event, held in "the foothills of Yosemite," was reputed to be feminist, uplifting, and orgiastic after dark. A place to meet women, to meet nature—a proper place for a modern, liberated lesbian, or even someone like me. Instantly I sent in a check.

The brochure used the words "camping" and "campsite" frequently, and in the section "What to Bring" listed (with uncharacteristic cruelty!) "the usual camping gear." These were mysterious words to me, since I had never once been camping. I'd spent my life in the dusty music practice rooms of school, then university, then home. I got out a pad of ruled paper and a pen to make a list and tried to imagine all the possible things "the usual camping gear" could entail. I guessed a tent was in order, also a sleeping bag.

I went to an upscale adventure store and bought a sleeping bag, a sleek black flashlight, and two citronella candles. The candles were packed in raffia and cost thirty dollars each. Looking around the store for more clues about camping, I spotted something I had always wanted. Now seemed the best time to purchase the shiny luggage cart of my dreams. I could use it for other trips as well. It felt sturdy, and my mood began to lighten.

After all, Hannah had never been to the Women's Music Festival. It was going to be an adventure all my own. And from stories I'd heard, romance—with a sweet, gentle, *natural* woman—was inevitable.

I got out my American Tourister and packed and repacked every weekend, practicing for the trip. My coffeemaker fit exactly into one corner, my hairdryer in another. I began to have fantasies, like literary flashbacks from a lesbian utopian novel, as the pile of camping items on my bedroom floor grew. I imagined glimmering golden light filtering through green meadows. At lakeside, women lounged like figures in a Renaissance tableau, some naked, slipping quietly into the blue water. Somewhere someone played a lute. I lay in a hammock, eating a fig. The glory of women, all ages and shapes and colors, drifted by, smiling at me.

I still needed a tent. I found the address of a sporting goods store in the yellow pages. I was nervous but determined. The clerk, a very young blond man, told me there weren't any tents left. Then he said wait, there was one, but he didn't know if I'd like it.

"It's a twelve-person tent," he said, leaning a long yellow roll against the counter.

"Okay!"

He smiled broadly as he leaned the tent toward me. It looked seven feet long. I dragged it through the store and people smiled. I felt outdoorsy and strong as I heaved it into my Toyota.

Hannah had been a good idea. Nothing will help you fit into a new community like hooking up with its central figure. In this case, it was Hannah, a solo lesbian geology professor wandering unfettered in the halls of the campus where I was recently hired as the cello instructor, where rumor had already spread that I was newly employed, new in town, lonely beyond belief.

It took only minutes of following her path one afternoon as she cut through the crowd of women celebrating the opening of the women's center to figure out how *powerful* she was. I pushed along in her wake, gearing myself up to introduce myself to her. I was counting on the rumor that Hannah had just left her partner and was momentarily unattached.

She approached the food table and my pulse quickened. What would I say? How to introduce myself to this woman, this *legend*? Whenever the other faculty—women and men alike—mentioned Hannah, their eyes grew wide, as if her name conjured an image so heady, so exhilarating.

"Hi," I squeaked to the round back, the stiff brown hair. Hannah turned and stuffed a cookie into her mouth. She was probably two feet taller than me, or so it seemed, and broader too. I said "Hi" again. Hannah threw her head back and laughed, a mahogany, alto laugh exposing pink sprinkles and capped teeth. She took my hand.

For some reason Hannah was smitten with me, and I was too relieved to wonder why. I know I made her laugh, which seemed important to her. Often enough I'd say something that gripped Hannah deep inside as the funniest thing she had ever heard. I almost never meant to be funny, and at first would chuckle uneasily with her, glad that she was entertained since I was falling in love with her. And then she would sense my unease and wrap a hand around some part of me, my knee, my hair, my waist.

It didn't take long to talk her into moving into my house; she seemed already packed, somehow. She filled my closets with cowboy boots and penny loafers. My pretty dresses were smushed against one wall while her dungarees and jackets took center stage. Her geology textbooks stood in ten precarious, totem-like piles throughout the house, always toppled by day's end. She snored. She left rings of dampness on my cello case. Twice she broke my eyeglasses: once knocking them to the floor and stepping on them in the usual course of her day; once when she grabbed me from behind, chewed on my neck, my glasses falling beneath her as we fell onto the carpet.

Time, too, presented conflicts. Hannah just didn't want to come to bed at night. She stood looking out the plate-glass window hour after hour. Sometimes she'd step outside onto the porch. Long after I had frowned myself to sleep, wondering why I hadn't fallen in love with someone who liked to cuddle, Hannah would appear in the threshold—it always woke me up—and fall into bed with a loud yawn. Then she would roll on top of me, growling and smelling of leaves.

Nearly every morning, the boulder of her sleeping form frightened me with its stillness. I would paddle out to the kitchen and drink two cups of tea, then come back into the bedroom and slither up between her breasts and arms, nudging up beneath her chin. Finally awakened, she would roll onto her back. I'd press my ear to the wide expanse of her belly, listening for signs of life.

She began to go out at night, further than the porch. First once a week, then more often than not. One morning after about a year of watching Hannah disappear yet again into the night, she announced from behind the morning paper that she was moving out.

I was gathering up my music books for the morning cello class and shook my head. "What?"

She lowered the paper, eyes black with determination, chewing on her thick bottom lip.

"Is there someone else?" I asked, an earthquake shimmying up my legs.

She nodded.

In the weeks after Hannah's departure, my little house grew cavernous. How could it be, I thought, that I felt whole before Hannah, and now half without her. Less than half. As if Hannah had inadvertently picked up my ego and packed it with her other belongings.

Every weekend I wallowed in disappointment, drinking scotch and playing over and over again the Bach concerto that Hannah loved most, the one that seemed to ease her body into the folds of the couch, turning her attention away from the front door and toward me. At the last note, she would stand behind me, leaning into my back, not noticing how icy drops of moisture from her glass landed on my scalp.

The morning I took off for my first camping trip, Hannah called. She was awkward, as usual, on the phone, and I had to—once I caught my breath—pry out of her why she was calling.

"How 'bout dinner tonight?" she mumbled.

"Sorry. Can't. I'll be out of town for three days."

Silence.

"At the Women's Music Festival." I swear I heard her gasp.

I hung up and checked my racing pulse. Why had she called? Was she in trouble? Did she need me? The phone rang under my hand. Hannah need me? I stared at the phone, stupefied. It stopped ringing. I picked up my luggage and went out to the car.

Bliss rose within me and kept rising as I locked up my little house in Burbank and drove out onto the highway, past the freeway system. The brochure guided my eighty-plus miles an hour onto a black highway striped in tangerine, fields of poppies the same hue, grass waving in the wind. I turned the cassette volume up as loud as it could manage and flew with the Brandenburgs across the San Joaquin Valley, the sun burning my elbow as it stuck out the window. I wore my favorite dress, and the dry hot wind blew beneath the pink cotton, through the sleeveless openings and down my neck, whirling around my bare ankles.

After a few hours, the directions grew more intricate. I resisted a few rises of panic. I tried to pay close attention to the words while keeping up the pace.

The feminist lesbians' twelve-page brochure's descriptions of small landmarks and significant signposts made me dizzy. "Watch for the mailbox painted like an American flag and slow down a little since you will eventually want to make a sharp right-hand turn after the fork in the road that butts up against a pasture where there are usually two cows and a bull."

Where were the traffic signals? And street signs? It grew hotter. I gripped the wheel as the landscape roughened. The brochure directions speeded up, grew more intense. Words like *be careful* dotted the remarks. The highway narrowed. Just as I thought I might be heading west instead of east, I passed a little wooden sign like a cross, painted with a woman's symbol and an arrow. I slowed down and turned onto the dirt road.

Axle banging into pits and over rocks, brown dirt swirling like a tornado, I and the Toyota arrived in the foothills of Yosemite, a vast dirt expanse desiccated into a desert by the unremitting California sun. I bounced to a stop at a shed where a few women stood around. The dust settled into cakes on the hood of my car. One of the women walked over and tapped on the window. She asked loudly if I had my ticket. I peered through the dust and saw that the women wore bluejean cutoffs and orange nylon vests, and for a moment I thought I had veered in the wrong direction at that last mailbox, ending up in the middle of a Caltrans road construction project.

"Your ticket?" the woman was almost shouting now. She must have thought I was hearing impaired. She swung a humungous flashlight in arcs—exercising, I supposed—while I dug through the glove compartment for the ticket.

"Am I at the Women's Music Festival?" I asked, noticing for the first time that she wore nothing beneath the vest. I quickly found my ticket.

"Sure are," she said, leaning her arms into my window, grinning. There was a little space between her two front teeth and she wore cherry-flavored Chapstick, I could smell it. She chewed her gum slowly a few times. Then the walkie-talkie on her hip squawked and she stood up abruptly, cleared her throat, and pointed. "Park your car there. Registration is just beyond the stand of eucalyptus."

I drove out into the middle of a dirt lot. There were some other cars, maybe ten or fifteen, so I pulled up next to them and parked. Fear rose suddenly into my throat but I took some deep breaths, told myself this was the hardest part, that soon I would find rest and refreshment and be watching the moon rise with thousands of other women, safe in the natural world.

My luggage cart would not cooperate. Every few steps in the soft dirt it tumbled over, once taking me with it. By the time I reached the registration shack, sweat streamed down my back and my glasses slid to the end of my wet nose. I had a pounding headache. My favorite pink dress was torn on one side.

The woman in the booth squinted in the sun. She wore a blue T-shirt soaked with sweat, no bra. Starting on the left side of her counter, she gathered up one flyer after another, a map of the campground and a bumper sticker that read I HEART WOMEN'S MUSIC.

The map of campsites looked like a cluster of grapes. One thick path led into the woods, and angling off from the path were the clearings. I held the map in one hand, pulling my luggage cart with the other, and made impossibly slow progress down the path.

I stopped at the first campsite marked by a white wooden post that said ALCOHOL FREE. Nope.

The next site, DRUG FREE, I thought, maybe, until I smelled the outhouse across and obviously upwind from the campsite. I had only used an outhouse once before, and I counted it as one of the top most unpleasant experiences of my life. Were there no toilets here? Nowhere?

CHILD FREE. Maybe. SMOKE FREE. Maybe. AROMA FREE. Huh? I was beginning to hope they had a zone just for me—DIRT FREE or even CAMP FREE. I was getting giddy with stress and hunger and thirst, and chose the next campsite, where there were already three or four tents and no signs.

I dragged the luggage cart, which by this time was on its side, the roll of tent sweeping along behind by a bungee cord, down the little slope into the clearing. I sat down on my suitcase and propped the tent between my legs. I unfurled the roll and as its considerable breadth began to intrude on the other nearby tents, several women crawled out to see what was going on.

"So sorry," I kept saying as they moved their cooking stuff, then their equipment, then dragged their tents to make room.

All the pieces duly laid out, I sat back down and read the instructions. I believe I could have figured it out if only there had been pictures, but there were none. Knowing I was being watched, I pulled my hammer from the suitcase (proud of myself to think of bringing along a tool), and proceeded to stuff long poles into sleeves of yellow and blue tent material. It was a pitiful performance, even in my estimation.

A shadow fell across my work.

"Hi there," said the shadow. I turned to look but the sunlight blinded me until the figure moved between me and the sun, and there stood a majestic woman, hands on hips, a string of what looked like animal teeth dangling between textbook-perfect bare breasts. "Need help?" She smiled then, displaying a dazzling row of perfectly aligned white teeth. A string of leather ran around her waist, her only clothing a rectangle of suede beaded with turquoise hanging from the leather thong. I was speechless.

She bent down to me, wide brown hands gently taking the hammer from mine, the little suede loincloth flapping in the breeze. Buck naked, she was, sun glinting off her flawless bronze skin.

"I'm Joan," she stated. She quickly fit together most of the tent. The teeth between her breasts jangled as she worked. "Expecting company?" she asked, propping up the final tent pole, her long thighs tensed, feet planted firmly in the earth. It didn't seem to matter to Joan that I was silent. She was probably used to women being struck dumb in her presence.

"Well, there you go. Have fun." She strode back to her tent, crouched down, reached inside and pulled out a bottle of beer. She took off up the path as if she had never worn a pair of shoes in her life.

Inside the eerie yellow tent, loneliness swelled into my throat. I took off my glasses and rubbed my temples. I paced the length of the nylon room, sipping from a bottle of Hannah's abandoned scotch, listening to women's laughter outside. Four warm ounces later, my stomach burning, the exigencies of a full bladder outweighed my intense desire to fall asleep and wake up somewhere else. I'd have to leave my empty, private, enormous yellow space. It took me a half hour to find my glasses, but at least they weren't broken.

I headed back up the path toward the outhouses. The outhouse was better than I expected and I reminded myself that there was no one but women here, as far as the eye could see. So many women, but not one of them Hannah. I made my way back to my tent, and sat inside dejectedly munching macaroons while the sun set.

I heard noises. The darkness was stunning when I unzipped the tent flap and went outside. Cold fresh air blew into my face. There were hundreds of women, it seemed, all heading one way up the path, clothed in parkas, gloves, and hats.

I went back inside and put on every dress I had brought. I was freezing. I put on another pair of socks and my jeans under my skirts, and followed the women, hoping there was some event that would distract me from my icy loneliness.

The hill formed a natural amphitheater, filled with outdoorsy women. As the moon rose, the emcee cleared her throat into the microphone.

"Welcome to the West Coast Women's Music Festival!" The audience hollered and whistled. I sat at the bottom of the hill, shivering at the sound and at the wind.

"Ladies," the emcee continued, tapping the mike and lifting her voice above screeching feedback, "we have some announcements."

The announcements were many and dire. Tics, apparently, were a special problem.

"So ladies, be sure to wash your hands...before *and* after." The women shrieked.

Two women's music acts later, the emcee called out that the lake was polluted—no swimming allowed. Yosemite had been on fire most of the year. Runoff of firefighting chemicals filled the lake, along with dangerous submerged debris. A disappointed "aaah" echoed from the hill.

The worst news came next.

"We have bear sightings, ladies," sang out the emcee. "This is no joke." My breath clutched in my chest.

A band behind the emcee, wanting to lighten the mood, began to play "Teddy Bears' Picnic"—our song, Hannah's and mine—and the starring act came out singing the lyrics with all her might. Everyone seemed to know the song, thousands of women gathered on the slope of a mountain, and the stars circled above our heads and I began to cry.

I would have gone back to my tent to drink myself to death, but I had forgotten to bring along my state-of-the-art flashlight. I had to wait until everyone decided it was time to go to sleep. Hours passed, filled with women's music and terrifying announcements about just how close the bears were getting.

"Ladies," called the emcee, tapping on the mike. "If you have any food in your tent, *get rid of it.* The bears are coming down. Don't even bother tying it up in a tree, the bears will smell it. We'll be sending people around to collect the trash barrels soon after the concert. Don't risk your life here by tempting those starving bears!"

I thought I would faint. Every time she said the word "bear" I ducked, as if they would fall from the trees right onto my head.

At last, the concert ended and I followed the beams of light down the path, luckily finding my tent. I grabbed the scotch and crackers and jar of caponata I had packed and ran full tilt to the trash barrel. Back inside, I zipped up the tent and considered praying for the first time in many years.

I heard others come into the campsite.

"Hey, Joan!" someone called. "Get this food out of here. You heard what they said about the bears."

"Ah, fuck the bears," Joan replied.

In the utter darkness and freezing cold, with nothing to drink or eat and an exhaustion soul-deep, I came to the irrevocable conclusion that this was the night of my death. I would be eaten by a bear and they would find little scraps of gnawed pink dress hanging from the trees. My only consolation was that Hannah would be deeply, deeply impressed.

Sometime far into the night it came. I heard the breaking twigs, the dislodged rocks chattering down the slope. Then grumbling sounds and huffing. I quit breathing as it approached my tent, leaves crunching on the other side of the thin fabric. I scrambled back against the farthest pseudo wall, the shadow weaving and looming. The growling became a moan and it seemed to lean on the tent, caving in the whole structure, pulling at the fabric beneath me, trying, I was sure, to yank me around closer for its first bite.

"Oh," said the bear. "Oh, baby."

The great shadow became an outline of elbows and knees, and Joan's unmistakable form. Joan and her paramour of the evening had apparently decided that in all of Yosemite, my tent was the perfect backdrop to their wild loving. I slunk down into the sleeping bag and passed out.

At dawn my eyes were swollen almost closed. I felt a zipper-shaped crease across my forehead and rubbed at it. Was it really Hannah that I missed, or was it something else? My house, my cello, the clean, safe order of my life? Surely that was an option, to stay at home, alone and safe. Surely bliss would drop by now and then, stay for tea or a drink, and then leave me to my own comfortable world. There had to be different ways to be modern and capable and natural in this world, different ways to be queer, and one of those ways was mine. I decided to go home.

Outside, I tore at the tent until it collapsed, then bound it up with bungee cords. My strength was superhuman as I carried the luggage cart, the tent, and my suitcase up the path. I still wore all my dresses. By this time in the morning, the rest of the three thousand campers had arrived and were waiting to register. They created a line down the length of the path like a gauntlet. As I worked my maniacal way past them to the parking lot, zipper mark still red across my forehead, each woman along the way in different stages of undress had nothing else to do but stare gape-mouthed at me.

"Are you leaving?" one called out, and everyone waited for a response. I pretended I couldn't hear.

When I got to the parking lot I paused. The lot shimmered in metallic light, filled bumper to bumper, door to door with thousands of cars, my Toyota somewhere dead center. I dropped my bundles. What to do? What to do?

"Hey there!" Joan thumped my back as she passed me on her way out to the lot.

"Joan!" I called after her. She wore still the same small piece of animal skin.

"What? What's this?" she cried, taking in my presentation. "Are you okay? Are you leaving? What's up? Do you have an emergency?"

"Yes, Joan. I have an emergency. I do. I really do. I need help. Will you help?"

Joan, suddenly enlightened, shoved my face between her breasts, pressing my body to her with her vast hands. The teeth in her necklace bit into my nose and I could feel my glasses bend. Her heartbeat pressed into my ear, it was all I could hear, though I think she was saying something. Or maybe just growling. Drool escaped from my mouth, she pressed me so hard. I smelled Obsession perfume and resisted the urge to stick my tongue out to catch a taste.

Then she let me go. I reeled.

"Where is your car? Give me your keys. We'll get you out of here, I promise." Her eyes darkened with severity.

"It's the silver Toyota with the scraped-up 'When All Else Fails Hug Your Teddy' bumper sticker," I told her, wincing at the truth.

"I understand," she said gravely, and took off for the center of the lot.

Two and a half hours later, every car in the lot had been square-danced around so that Joan could drive right up to where I stood. She gallantly opened the door.

"In you go!"

I got in, closed the door with a bang and locked it. I drove fast, careening and bumping out of the lot. Joan waved gracefully in the rearview mirror.

Finally out on the road, I shoved in a cassette of Bach concertos and rolled down the window. In a flurry of wind a beige bit of paper flew onto the dashboard. It was a business card. *Northwoods Tavern,* it read, *twenty percent off weekdays,* and in the spaces between the print was scrawled *Joan Goldstein* and a phone number. I puzzled most of the way home where she had been carrying the card.

🐚

Twice a year I make the drive down to Long Beach to have a beer. Northwoods Tavern is right by the beach, but it's built like a log cabin, its plaster roof painted white and shaped like snow. Joan wears a short brown uniform that shows off her legs. There's always a bowl of peanuts on the table. Joan taught me to drop the empty shells onto the sawdust-covered floor. I watch her wait on tables and toss the shells her way. At the end of her shift, we go back to her apartment. For three hours we are impassioned and athletic. I am exhausted and sticky all over and smell of peanuts and beer and Obsession and the ineffable saltiness of Joan's hidden places. I am filled with bliss.

Every so often, though, Joan holds onto my fingers longer than necessary as we say goodbye. I can feel the tug, but I am a modern, liberated lesbian and I recognize wild things when I see them, luscious but dangerous. I am no longer a fool. Hannah has had a number of lovers since our parting, a hunger driving her out into the night. Joan, loving and strong, has the smell, too, of leaves about her, of leaving.

Those nights after seeing Joan, when I'm at home alone in my small, clean house, I drop off to sleep easily, sweetly, but it does not last. Those nights, invariably, I dream of bears.

Floating By

This is what I am thinking while being interviewed for a job at the Howard Johnson's: according to my mother, it used to be that a hotel restaurant was a classy place where the idle wives of wealthy men spent lots of money. These women and their teenage daughters wore fox stoles and pillbox hats, and long white gloves they pulled off finger by finger as you served them Waldorf salad. My mother was a waitress, and her mother before her. I've been at it now for a bunch of years. Not a very illustrious lineage, except for those grand old hotels.

I'll bet the waitresses running around here like mad don't feel like this is a classy joint. Not by a long shot.

"How old are you?" says the young man who's interviewing me.

I know he is not supposed to ask that, but I don't say anything, because I really need the job, having been let go with everyone else when the new owners of Ruby's decided they wanted a younger staff.

"Well, probably older than you." I smile at him, but he just looks down at the form he's filling out. While he writes, I remember the last time my son and I shared a burger here. Sandy had just gotten some award from junior high, guess I should remember what it was for, but all I remember is how tired I was from working back to back shifts at Ruby's.

"Thanks for coming in today, Mrs. Jones," the young man says, rising, still not looking me in the eye.

"Call me Sunny!"

"Well, Sunny, thank you. We'll be calling soon."

He never calls. But, lucky for me, there is an opening at Phillip's Chicken Pie Shop, and the new owner, Tuan, likes me. Tuan tells me he is Vietnamese. We sit on hard folding chairs as he says that when he bought this place the gal who had waitressed here for years didn't want to work for an Oriental. Then he shows me a photo of his other restaurant, a sushi bar in Koreatown in Los Angeles.

It is a photo of customers seated around a circular counter. Tuan explains how the counter has a trough cut into it, and water flows in a steady stream round and round the counter. The chef stands in the middle, chopping fish and placing it on little wooden planks that float right past each customer's plate.

"I name it Floating By. See how the sushi float by?" He slaps my knee, laughing. Then he waves his hand around us, at the cooler, and the walls and the floor of the restaurant.

"Maybe I call this place Floating Pie! How 'bout that? Just kidding!" He doubles over with laughter, tears streaming from his eyes. What a nice guy.

He changes the name of the place to Floating By because he's starting a "big American chain." The day I start the job Tuan is up on a ladder, painting over the pie shop name with red paint.

I keep waiting for Tuan to turn the restaurant into a sushi bar, but it never happens, and I'm glad. I don't like fish much. All we serve are pot pie dinners. And there is a lot to be said for serving the same people the same thing day in and day out: chicken pot pie. We have turkey pot pie twice a year, but mostly it's just chicken pot pie, all day long. I like that.

It has been Phillip's Chicken Pie Shop for so long that most of my customers are older than me by three decades. Which makes them pretty old.

I think it's kind of funny that a Vietnamese person is running the show, but everything is going okay. The same folks are coming in. The tips are good enough. So I'm not sure why Tuan hired the new waitress. I'm hoping like heck it's not because he thinks I'm too slow or something. I mean, I'm fast enough for these old folks.

On the other hand, Zappa, the new waitress, is like lightning. Gosh, those coffee cups are always filled up and still she seems to have time to smoke a cigarette about every fifteen minutes. But I did find out she has her problems. Toward the end of her first lunch run, I find her in the storage room crying over a pile of tickets.

"Honey, don't cry. It's not brain surgery."

"I can't get these straight," she shrieks and then she falls into my arms. I kind of stumble back because Zappa is a big girl, plump. But then I catch my balance and pat her back. I can feel her earrings digging into my neck. She has four in each ear, running up the flap like little red ants.

"I'll do it," I tell her. "Don't cry." She straightens up and rubs her eyes. I take all her tickets and add them up. "Here you go."

It's like the sun coming out, then: Zappa's tears dry up and she grins. She is pretty when she smiles, even though her hair is the color of black shoe polish and she has pimples on her fat cheeks. It's nice to see a little padding these days when all the girls are so horribly skinny. I guess she's about twenty or so, like Sandy. I wonder if Sandy is eating okay.

"I hate numbers," she says.

I wonder if she's one of those girls who talked her way into the job, you know, lied about some experience in some other town with streets like Main and Broadway. Old Town Café on Main Street. How many of those are there? Zillions, I bet.

I'm surprised each day how glad I am to see Zappa when she shows up at Floating By. It's nice to have her around. I think that's why Tuan hired her, just for the company or the noise. There are only the two of us because the baker works at night. I don't know if Tuan has any family. I never see any. He doesn't look that old to me. He's a skinny little thing with great big brown eyes that he levels at Zappa when she's in the back lighting up.

Even though Zappa is Sandy's age, we get along really well, mostly because she makes me laugh all day making faces and rolling her eyes when she thinks her customers aren't looking or are too blind to focus on her face. But also I think she's kinda lonely. I don't really know much about her; like Tuan, she never mentions any family. She's private, which is fine with me. But one day when we're in the storage room counting our tips, she lets out a few things about herself.

"Ice cream."

That look on her face! It has "yum" written all over it.

"What kind?"

"All kinds. Can't get enough of it." Maybe this explains her bad skin.

"Well, why don't I come over to your place sometime and bring some ice cream and we can play cards?" I'm a little surprised at myself, inviting myself over like that. But I need the company. Since Sandy left, I'm watching way too much TV.

Sandy would like Zappa, I think. Or maybe he wouldn't. It's harder and harder to tell what my green-eyed son likes, although I know he quit liking me at about age thirteen. I didn't take it too personal, though, since boys get surly at around that time, what with all the hormones and everything. All the boys in his little group at school got shifty-eyed and snarly, and while some of the other moms paid for therapists, I just let Sandy slam doors. That's what I could afford.

I have to admit I was a little surprised, though, two years ago when he called from Missoula. He was supposed to be at his high school prom at Disneyland—expensive tickets, those were. I don't know how he got to Missoula. I don't even know where Missoula is. And I don't even know why he called me, because all he did was act mad and hang up on me.

Zappa writes her address on a blank ticket and shoves it into my pocket.

Zappa lives in the Dolores Hotel. The hotel sits at the foot of Signal Hill, across from two oil derricks. I brought Sandy to the top of the hill once to watch the sun set way out over the ocean. It was prettier then. Now the pollution makes it all gray. Unless there's a fire in the mountains. Then the sunsets are wild.

I'm nervous walking up to the hotel because it's dark and I'm alone. There's a white wooden door, and then a carpeted stairway with wide stairs. It smells a little off, like mold and urine. I climb three flights and knock.

"Who's there?" Zappa calls through the closed door.

"Sunny."

Locks come loose, bolts slide back and keys click before the door opens.

"Hey there." Zappa smiles. "Come on in."

"I brought ice cream."

Zappa takes the paper bag from me with one of her yum smiles. "Lock the door behind you, will you?" she calls over her shoulder from the table where she divides the gallon of Neapolitan in half into enormous fake wooden bowls. "The landlord has been giving me grief."

"What's he doing?"

Zappa motions to the couch, the only substantial piece of furniture in the one-room apartment. The couch is covered with a granny knot afghan.

"He wants me to have sex with him," she says. "I'm asking $200, but if I quit Floating By, I might settle for fifty."

I'm a little shocked at this information, but Zappa seems casual enough about it. She tells me she's getting bored with her job. "There are just too many old geezers with cabbage all over their face, you know what I mean?"

I sort of do. Like sometimes I feel sorry for my customers. Most of them are old men and they're single and you can tell they need caring for. They smell musty and their hands are dirty and their fingernails too long. They mostly come from the rest home up the street.

"Zappa, honey, do you really think you should quit? I mean, what will you do for money?"

She lowers her chin and sighs. "Anyway, the thing is, Sunny, I've got to see what's out there. You know, before it's too late."

"Too late? Too late for what?"

"Oh, never mind," she says. I feel bad, like I should say something to cheer her up, but she starts clearing away the bowls so I figure it's time to go.

The next lunch shift Zappa shows up, but she pulls Tuan into the back room, I guess to tell him she's quitting. I'm just setting down two pies when I hear them yelling and think I'd better go help out.

"You have to stay!"

"No way, José. I don't have to do *jack*."

"What are you saying?" Tuan is wringing his hands. "Who is Jack?"

So I say, "Zap, why don't you just stick around for a while, until you find something else?"

"No! You can't make me stay!"

What a strange thing for her to say, as if she's in prison or something instead of at her job. I think she may have lost her marbles. Or maybe she took some drugs. She looks like she's about to cry, so I kinda reach out to hug her.

Well, this works like magic. She slumps into my arms and says, "Okay, I'll stay for a week," and Tuan smiles. Crikey, what a handful. Tuan is all calmed down, so I go out to take care of my customers, who suddenly seem like a lot less work.

I visit Zappa again. I do think it's a little strange she doesn't have friends her age. But then, well, neither do I.

The locks click open and there she is. I hand her the gallon of fudge ripple and bring the sack of groceries I brought to the table. We sit on the couch again.

"I'm making extra money on the side. Look." She reaches around the back of the sofa, bringing an old blanket onto her lap. "Horse blankets. I'm sewing horse blankets. One dollar a pop."

I can't imagine how she got hold of the blankets, or who would pay for such a thing. There aren't any horses around here at all. Used to be. Not anymore. I tell Zappa, "When I was little, my mom took me to ride a pony at the Pike. I was scared to death."

Zappa is watching the door, slumped happily on the couch, swirling her spoon around the bowl. She seems awfully mysterious for such a young gal.

"Where're your folks, hon?" I ask.

"They're around, I guess. My dad's around here, anyway."

"And your mom?"

"Palm Springs, I think." Zappa shrugs. "I left home a long time ago."

I feel a pang at that. Sandy hasn't called for two months. Usually it's just a few weeks between calls. I guess it's because the last phone call we had we argued. He said it was all my fault. Everything. But I don't see that there was all that much wrong with his world. So his dad left when he was a kid. So I had to work all the time. Really, is that so terrible? I mean, he always had food. Always. When I pointed that out, he yelled, "That's what you always say! Why don't you get it?" So I said, "Get what?" and he hung up.

"Why'd you leave?" I ask Zappa. She doesn't answer, so I figure she will when it's something I need to know about her. She seems levelheaded but you never know what's hurting someone. As we sit eating the ice cream, I picture Sandy and Zappa holding hands, walking into the Breakers Hotel in its swanky days. His hair is too long, but healthy, like his skin. And Zappa's hips sway back and forth. They are celebrating something, like graduating from high school, or college, or getting a raise or getting married. Something, anyway.

"Sandy isn't really speaking to me, Zappa. I don't know where he is." This comes out of me before I know it and I cough and wipe my eyes, but Zappa just shrugs.

On Sunday I drive by the Dolores Hotel on my way to Costco, and there is Zappa sitting on the bus bench. On her lap is a mannequin's leg. She spots me and waves the plastic leg in the air. I pull up and roll down the window.

"Hey, Sunny! What are you doing here?" She grins. "Just in time! Can you give me a ride downtown?"

She hops in, tossing the leg into the back seat, and I u-turn to go back downtown.

"What is that?"

"Extra earnings, Sun. I've got plans. Can you take me to Buffums?"

I wonder what on earth Zappa wants at that old ladies' store. Buffums has been an old ladies' store since I was a kid, and it just sits on Pine Avenue, watching downtown get all spruced up with neon.

"I met this couple. They want me to sell their stockings. Look. They're called Diamond Legs." Zappa wrestles the leg onto the front seat between us. It has an orangish nylon on it with little sequins in the shape of a diamond sewn onto the ankle. "I'll probably sell enough to buy a ticket out of here."

"But where will you go?"

I know Zappa is a rambling kind of gal, but I don't want her to leave. She doesn't answer, and as I drive around I think of all the places Sandy has been to. Last night he finally called, and the phone call was actually a good one. He had a new plan, not that I was aware that he had an old one. I don't know what my son is doing. All I know is now he's in Santa Fe. That's always the first thing I ask. Where are you now?

"Mom, I'm in school."

Okay, I could hardly believe my ears. "Really?"

"Yep. The Bartending College."

I wanted to ask him when he was coming home. But I couldn't, because before, when he called from Denver, I had asked him that and he launched into a tirade about how he didn't know where home was, and that it certainly wasn't with me, because after all he hadn't asked to be born, hadn't asked for all this misery. So I got mad back and said, listen, Sandy, what misery are you actually referring to? Then he yelled stupid things like me not respecting him, not thinking he was worth anything. Honestly, where he gets those ideas, I don't know. All I ever said to my son was how beautiful he was. And how sweet. Well, until he turned thirteen. Then I called him a sourpuss. Big deal. Boo hoo. How was I supposed to know it would hurt his feelings like that? How sensitive can a kid be?

So I was being extra careful with this conversation to not make him mad. "Bartending! Okay!"

"Mixology. Highballs. Shooters. I'm taking a special course in flair. Flipping jiggers and whatnot."

I pictured my son in a saloon in New Mexico, his hair tied back, a white shirt with garters holding back the sleeves. His green eyes light up when Zappa saunters in, her ample body corseted and swaying side to side.

"I'll bet you're really good, son."

"Okay. Gotta go. Call ya in a week or something."

The promise of another call makes me pretty happy as I drive Zappa downtown.

"I used to work there," she says, pointing at La Playa, a Mexican place just opposite Buffums. "My boss was my best friend for a while. Her name was Bell, isn't that pretty? She was older, too."

She stares out at the restaurant like she wants to just sit there and think about La Playa all day long, but cars are honking at me because I'm double-parked, so I pull away.

I turn right on Ocean Boulevard, which leads further away from the good part of town, but I like to drive along the bluff starting way up on the northern edge of Long Beach.

"As soon as I get enough money … " Zappa says, gazing out the window.

"But why?" What is it with these young people, floating from place to place, leaving great towns like Long Beach, with its nice weather and the beach and all?

"Drive down there, okay?" Zappa waves her hand over at the Queen Mary, the ship unmoving, cemented into its man-made marina. "I hate palm trees. Someone told me rats sleep in them at night. I believe that."

I head down the street, down to the beach and up through some complicated on-ramps until we hit the Queen Mary parking lot.

"I used to work there," she says, pointing up through the car window to the tip of the ship. "Up there, in the Observation Bar. I served cocktails. I had no experience at all so I got the orders all messed up. Plus the people who go there are all tourists who don't feel the need to tip. Not that I deserved it. It was a hell job, I'll tell you that. I barely made enough for the cab home."

"A cab? That's expensive."

"The bus doesn't come out here at night."

I think about Zappa in a cocktail waitress uniform climbing into a yellow taxi in the middle of the night. That is a terrible thought.

"Zappa, honey, don't you miss your mom?"

Zappa is distracted by the ship, and doesn't seem interested in answering. But she finally turns to me, and I think she might be on the verge of tears. "Listen, can we just drive around?"

"Don't you have an appointment at Buffums?"

"Nah."

I drive back to Ocean Boulevard and head south along the bluff. We pass the Long Beach Museum of Art and those steep steps leading down to the beach, so I tell Zappa about holding hands with my mom when I was a kid going down those scary steps, and then years later holding little Sandy's hand. He wasn't scared at all.

"Neat," is all she says.

We wander around for an hour, hopscotching to all the places Zappa has ever worked, which seems to be one of every kind of restaurant you can find in Long Beach: coffee shops, little neighborhood cafés, fast food. I can't believe how often Zappa's just up and quit. She tells me she was trying to leave town, but never had enough money. In each job she was unhappier than the last. She hates California. The Santa Ana winds give her hives. The sun gives her headaches. And she says the salty, sticky marine air makes her feel like a deflated balloon.

"There's poor people, begging people, crazies everywhere, Sunny. Why stick around a sad place like this?"

"Is it sad?" I ask, looking out over the bluff at the seagulls soaring like kites above the ocean. I park the car and we roll down all the windows, and the sea breeze whips waves into Zappa's hair.

I know the city has grown dusty, smelling like gasoline and red tide more often than not, but the sky can't be matched for blueness and there is never a day when a walk is difficult due to bad weather. But it's more than that: I tell Zappa there is a peace here, a stillness here that comes from the sea, from all that sun-warmed sand. She just shrugs.

"My dad likes it here, too," she says, resting her head on the back of the seat. "But then, he's pretty easy to please."

"And your mom?"

Zappa blushes and I think, okay, now I'm going to hear something that's gonna make me cry. But she shakes the thought away and turns her grin to me.

"Last year my name was Caitlin." She laughs, but I'm alarmed. What does she mean? "I pretended I was Irish. I ate nothing but potatoes."

"That's a little crazy, Zap." Where on earth are her parents? How can they just let her go? But then suddenly it occurs to me that maybe some older gal somewhere in the southwest is listening to Sandy complain, and is coming to the same conclusion about me. That I'm an awful mother. The worst mother in the whole world. This makes me so mad I want to pound the steering wheel. I am not that bad. I'm just not. I am very relieved when Zappa interrupts my thoughts.

"I'm hungry. Let's just go eat, okay?"

We end up at the Northwoods Tavern in Belmont Shore, Zappa's idea. It's nice and dark and cool in here. The waitress is slow, though. She's hanging out with a friend over at the table by the jukebox. We have to wave to get her attention. After she leaves with the menus and our order, Zappa says, "Look. They're lovers." She's pointing to the waitress, who is back at the table with the friend. I guess Zappa is right, the way the two gals are blinking real slow at each other. Well, in this world, I can kind of understand it.

"Men do break gals' hearts."

"Oh, I disagree, Sunny. It's the women who'll do it to you."
She stares out into the darkness of the restaurant, and I guess I
don't really need to know the specifics. There it is, her broken
heart. Thank god our ice cream finally arrives.

"How much money do you need before you can leave?" I
ask over a dish of rocky road. The plastic leg sits next to us in its
own chair.

"Fifty bucks will buy me a one-way Greyhound ticket."

"To where?"

"I'm thinking New Orleans. I think I can make some money
there."

I don't ask Zappa doing what. Or why New Orleans. She has
already explained that the landlord got what he wanted, for $79
and change. I wonder if she's told her mother. Now there's a way to
break a woman's heart. When I tell Zappa as much, she says, "But
my mom doesn't care, Sunny. She's busy. A very busy person. She
calls me a vagabond. My dad says that's a compliment." She pauses
and looks around at the waitress and her friend. "She should talk.
You know what she named me? Toby. Can you believe that? What
kind of a name is that? Maybe she wanted me to run off and join
the circus." Zappa smiles. "Maybe I have."

"Zappa, speaking as a mother here, I have to say, there is no
way she hates you. No way."

She shrugs. "You don't see Sandy."

"Because he's always mad at me."

"For what?"

I want to say, for no good reason, but I only half believe that. There has to be a reason. Maybe it's just me, the kind of mother I am. Instead, I say, "Your guess is as good as mine, honey."

Zappa digs deep into the bowl and brings up a big scoop of ice cream. She licks the outside edges of it, smiling. She shrugs again, and I think the conversation is probably over, but I want to ask her one more thing.

"Zappa, what should I say to Sandy? What should I say to bring him home?"

Zappa leans over the table toward me then, pulls both my hands into hers, and says, "Sunny. I am so sorry but you are so asking the wrong person."

I keep waiting for Sandy to call. Finally, a week later, he does. I turn down the volume on the TV.

"Where are you?"

"Flagstaff." He sounds angry, and I wonder what's coming next. "Why do you always ask me that?"

"What, where you are?"

"I mean, what business is it of yours?" He starts in on me. While he begins numbering all his frustrations—no work, no friends, no this, no that, it all being my fault because he didn't ask to be born—I watch a show about Dixieland jazz musicians in New Orleans, watch them silently swing their clarinets back and forth.

"Excuse me," I say. "I'm sorry."

"What?" Sandy sounds surprised, a little squeak at the end of the "what?" that I haven't heard since he was a child.

"I'm sorry," I say again, and then I start to sniffle. I ask him if he'll come home, and he says he doesn't know, but he gives me his address anyway. He hangs up before I say *I love you*. The phone is warm under my palm as I try to remember the last time I said that to him. When? When? I can't even remember and my heart sinks.

It's been three weeks now, and I am so worried about Zappa I can hardly stand it. Tuan is worried too, I think. After we lock up, we sit together while he eats a sweet-smelling soup and I count my tips and I notice him looking around, just gazing around as if he's never seen this place before. As if he is in a foreign country and is not sure he likes it.

Every night I watch TV and eat Neapolitan ice cream. I'd be fat as heck if it weren't for Floating By keeping me on my feet all day long.

But finally, finally, I get a postcard from Zappa. It's a picture of an island and the little type on it reads, "Puget Sound, Washington State."

I turn the card over. Zappa's written on it: "I got a job on a fishing boat! I make a lot of money! Changed my name to Rain. Hope you are okay. Write back, okay? Please?"

Rain. I can't even imagine that, changing her name again.

A few days later, Sandy walks into Floating By and the pie I'm serving slips off the plate onto the table. I ignore the mess and throw my arms around my son, who is standing tall and skinny in the middle of the restaurant.

We hug for a long minute until my customer says, "I can't eat off the table. What the hell is going on?"

Sandy balls up his fists, but I push him toward the counter. Tuan rushes past me with a wet rag. My son sits at the counter while I serve some more pie. He points at the postcard I got from Zappa that I taped to the cash register and calls out, "What's this, Mom?"

My heart does a little jig at that, hearing *Mom* across the restaurant. I just stop right where I am and burst into tears. Tuan comes over and pulls me toward the counter and pours us all coffee.

By the time we finish our first cup, Tuan offers Sandy a job baking at night.

"Pie pie pie," he says. "All night long. How 'bout that?"

Sandy shrugs then, just like Zappa—I mean Rain—used to. Tuan smiles.

I lean against Sandy and wrap my arms around him, pull him against my pounding heart, and look over his shoulder at the postcard of the blue blue water. I think about Zappa on a cold wet boat, alone, and I want to write back, right away, and say I think you should come back here and be with me and Sandy and Tuan because anything is possible. I always think that: anything is possible. Anything at all.

Acknowledgments

I'm grateful to the following people/entities: Cottages at Hedgebrook, for a month-long writing retreat; Rosalie Morales Kearns, for her vision and editorial guidance; my many short-story mentors, you know who you are; my few and dear first readers, you know who you are; and the talented and hilarious Sean Finucane Toner, for everything.

About the Author

Robin Parks is originally from Southern California, where she grew up in poverty. She spent most of her twenties waiting on tables in the Long Beach area, including a stint at Egg Heaven on 4th and Ximeno. She then lived on tiny Lummi Island, Washington, finally settling in Bryn Mawr, Pennsylvania. She has an M.F.A. from Fairleigh Dickinson University, where she was the Presidential Fellow in Creative Writing, and her fiction has won the Raymond Carver Short Story Award. She is the fiction editor of *Referential Magazine* (referentialmagazine. org).